Prologue

Hope breeds eternal disappointment. I love that quote. It's so refreshing and real, a break from the "hang in there's" and the "if you can dream it, you can achieve its" of today's fake positivity movement. Why give people false hope, when all that gives you in return is let down after let down?

I'm not a remarkable person. In fact, I'm quite remarkably unremarkable. I'm not talented at anything, but rather extremely talented at achieving mediocrity in everything I've tried. It's frustrating. In fact, I'm average. So when you say to the average person like me "if you can dream it you can achieve it", I'll wake up in the morning bleary eyed, stumbling around in the dark to get ready to go to my average job, where I'll spend the whole day fighting back the urge to walk out, but I have to pay my rent so..But oh, I'll be dreaming alright.

Disappointment. Constant disappointment is my life. Or was.

As you've probably gathered, I'm not a very positive person. Well, I can be but I'm just a realistic person. "I'll believe it when I see it", "don't take me for a mug" kind of person. Funny thing is, deep down, I'm quite the opposite. I like to look for real magic in things, coincidences and the like. What if that kind of stuff were true? I mean destiny, a higher path, a bigger purpose. I'm actually full of hope, brimming with hope, bursting with hope even. Always thinking to myself that one day I'll be proved right. I'll be able to lift away the mask that's been hiding my true naïve self, and exclaim: You see ! It does exist! You fools! I'm the fool. I've wasted so much time and energy hoping.
Do I regret thinking like that? No

After many ups and downs in my life, most of them too dull to report on, I found myself in my mid-twenties living alone in a rented house. A house I had shared for three years previously with my ex-boyfriend. This was my second long term relationship, the first of which had ended on a sour note but is what brought me to meet my second long term partner. Carlos was just what I needed, fun, kind, caring. We met and hit it off, and within a couple of months he had moved in, and we started our journey together. I was always one to get carried away, swept off my feet at the very thought of being swept off my feet.

Once passion was there, I was there, and it felt so right. You know that feeling when you can't breathe you want somebody so much? Every fibre of your being aches, physically aches for this person, and you want to breathe them in forever. That's what passion is for me. That's why I love the start of relationships. All that "head in the clouds" fuzziness, that's my favourite. Carlos and I settled together and as life continued on and jobs came and went, we were pretty happy. After a couple of years, I started to feel a shift in our relationship, the passion had fizzled out and the talk had fizzled out. We each came to have our own separate lives. Him working at night and me working during the day. We would pass each other in the house briefly from time to time, but that's the routine we settled at. I knew things weren't going to change, and I knew we wouldn't work at it to change. We parted ways. He finally moved out and there I was, happy to be with myself again, to find myself again
.

I had forgotten how much I liked having my own space, my own company. I didn't realise until much later, but I've always been an introvert. Living alone was great, I did what I liked when I liked. My confidence grew. I didn't depend on anyone to tell me if I looked good, I simply felt good, and it was so liberating.

After a few weeks I was ready to give myself a change of scenery. I got a new job. There were so many new people but with my new confidence I wasn't scared. I was happy to change, it was exciting. I made some new friends and was generally happy. It was like a breath of clean fresh air. Sam was one of my best friends there. She shared my sense of humour, and we would find ourselves laughing so hard we had tears rolling down our red faces. She always insisted I join her on nights out with our colleagues and at first, I wasn't eager. When the day at the office was finally at an end, I loved to just go home and close the door behind me. Unwind. She preferred to go relax with a drink or two. As time passed and I had been single for about a year, a loneliness crept in. A yearning for affection and human contact . I decided it was time to try dating.

I was always considered a pretty girl. People called me pretty. When I was younger, I never had any problems getting boyfriends. I have blue eyes and brown dark hair, I'm petite . I had always gotten looks when walking down the street or in bars but now it seemed men didn't approach me at all. I couldn't understand why.
Wanting to be with someone so much and it not happening created a sense of pressure and overwhelming desperation that I can't begin to describe. Each passing day thinking about why I hadn't met someone and what was it going to take and what was happening here. Each passing day leading me to obsess about it even more. Wishing and hoping that the next night out would be the night, and then it not happening all over again became unbearable. My confidence in turn took a knock. I understood much later that the root, or should I say, little seedling of depression had already started its germination in my head.

The darkness grew. Even more time passed. I was frustrated, exasperated and confused. What was wrong with me? I didn't *need* a man, I didn't *need* to be validated, but I craved intimacy. The countless bars and clubs, the same drunk men, the same friends regaling in the company of their prospective suitors, and me. Alone.

The darkness consumed me and while I didn't know it at the time I was spiralling. I had been alone for two years and I wasn't happy or content with my job any longer. I just wasn't happy anymore. Nothing brought me any fulfilment.

One particular night and going out with   friends, I was feeling excited. Despite my rock bottom self-confidence, I convinced myself it was going to be a great night. I got home from work and started to get ready, picking out my clothes and doing my hair and makeup, just trying to be happy. It was Friday night and Summer. The sky was blue, and the air was warm. Once I was ready and somewhat satisfied with my outfit, I hopped into a taxi and made my way into the city centre to meet Sam. We met up and made our way to the bar to meet the rest of our group of colleagues and my spirits were high. You know that feeling when there's a buzz in the air, there's an electricity you can
feel around you? When I feel that it feels like magic is alive, like something amazing is going to happen, something fantastical. The wind feels different, the air is charged, changes are happening.

I felt that everything was aligning. The positive change I had been waiting for was in sight. The planets were in place. The mood was right, and I felt good. Tonight, was the night. I would have bet my arm. I really would have.

At the end of the night, as I walked down the empty dark cobble stoned street alone to catch my taxi home, there had been no change. There had been no magic. There had been nothing. How could I have been so stupid? How could I have been so idiotic to think that I could *feel* change or that something magical was going to happen? Grow up for fuck's sake, look at how pathetic you are, just pathetic. It had
been the last drop and I overflowed.

In the taxi I sobbed. Stop feeling so fucking sorry for yourself, you're such a fucking loser. My inner voice. Who would want to be with someone like you you fucking ugly bitch? And I sobbed some more.
"Would you like a tissue?" came a man's voice.

"No thanks" I mumbled, realising I was in a stranger's taxi and that perhaps it would be best to cry at home.

After that night it was hard. It was hard to be excited about doing things. It was hard to be around people. I avoided going out so that I could avoid disappointment. I avoided everything and everyone. I quit my job, I moved away. I convinced myself that I was unhappy because of these things. I just wanted to be gone, be invisible, start fresh.

There is a part of the story so far that I've left out. That's because it's about 60 seconds of my life. But those 60 seconds are the start of my story.

Chapter 1

It was the start of another night out, one in the string of many. I was sinking deeper and deeper into my pool of self-loathing and bitterness. I still had my head just above the water though.

It was the start of Summer. The air was crisp, but the sun was shining. The days were getting longer. I had just met up with a colleague and we were making our way to the pub where the rest of the group were waiting.

"Do you know where this pub is?" I said.

"I think so" she said not sounding too confident.

"Are you sure?" I said.

"Oh wait it's not down here, mm, maybe it's down this street" she said.

Neither of us knew where this bar was. I didn't because I hardly knew the city and I never wanted to go out. It was a rare moment for my colleague who knew the city like the back of her hand. We made our way up one street and down another, convinced the bar would be just around the next corner. No luck. We were both in a giggly mood anyway. The sun shone; we weren't in a hurry.

"Maybe it's down here" she said.

We walked up a smaller street, a lane more like. Artists' studios to either side, a cobble stoned street. Chatter and buzz spilled out onto the sidewalk.

"It doesn't look like there are any pubs here" she said as we rounded the top of the street. I could see a man standing up ahead with his back turned.

"Maybe that guy knows" she said. I shrugged my shoulders and followed her towards him.

"Excuse me" she said, and the man turned around to face us. He had just been lighting a cigarette, his face huddled away, presumably so that the wind wouldn't blow out his flame. His hair was dark and curly, messy. He had a camera in his hand. I looked at him, but not his face. His eyes. I looked directly into his eyes. I don't know why. He looked into mine. I heard my friend, muffled, "do you know where this bar is?" Still looking into his eyes and him in mine and without breaking our connection, he answered "no".
 It was a surprised no. I wasn't aware of the world around me, my colleague forgotten. I didn't know who I was or where I was in that moment. I was in a blur; I had no sense of time. Our eyes locked. Time passed, and I became aware of my friend saying "c'mon!   " and tugging at my coat sleeve.

She pulled me, and as my legs began to walk away, our eyes tore themselves apart from one another's. Still walking and being pulled, I turned my head back. I saw him at the top of the street looking down. We found the bar and got on with our night.

His brown eyes, I can see them now in my mind's eye. Warm pools. Enveloping. Safe. Like our souls had recognised each other, like somehow our inner selves had had a conversation with each other that we on the outside were not aware of.

In my life I had never had a connection like that with someone. These 60 seconds became a part of me as time passed and was still something I thought about. Sometimes regularly, sometimes now and then and sometimes with regret. Sometimes with acceptance that it would always stay just a nice moment, a frozen fragment in time that had no past and no future, and that I was lucky somehow to have experienced.

Was I reading too much into it? I had a tendency to do that, as you know. What if this person forgot about me the second I walked away. What if this magic wasn't shared. I knew if I saw him again even years later, I would remember him. Would he remember me? What if he didn't? That would prove me foolish and break me I think - if I recognised him and he didn't. Would I prefer to not know and keep that memory untouched, or to know once and for all? I was curious more than anything. Curious if I was in fact foolish, if I saw things where there was nothing, or if I saw meaning where there simply wasn't any.

When my real life wasn't going so well it gave me a momentary exit, an escape, a fantasy. Daydreaming of being special, of someone feeling the same as I. We had our little secret and we were the only two people in the world who knew about it.

Chapter 2

Moving into my new apartment distracted me. I was closer to my childhood home and starting my new job. Getting settled, I loved decorating and making it my own. I was content with my decision to move and eager for this change to take me in a new direction.

 As the dust settled, literally and figuratively, routine set in and my old pattern began to remerge. Slowly but surely the distraction wilted away, and I was left with my thoughts once more. Sadness, anger, frustration. I hated the job, and I hated the people. It slowly hacked away at me. I began crying myself to sleep every night. I would wake up and for a second, I would be numb, then I would remember where I was and who I was and what my life was and my body would tremble and shake and sob. My inner voice became harsher and harsher. I didn't realise it then, this was full blown depression. I had no idea. I just knew it was getting worse and worse.

I chopped off my long hair, I got another tattoo. Anything to change things. I would try something and say, this is going to work, I needed a new look, I needed a change, that was all. Nothing worked. I turned into somebody I didn't recognise. I had left my body and I was a shell. I could feel no joy, no matter the situation. I was perpetually grey. I went away for a couple of weeks thinking a holiday would be good. I hardly spoke a word the entire time and couldn't bring myself to smile or laugh or ta ke part in life. I could feel that I wanted to, I wanted this shroud to be removed. I wanted this weight, this darkness to be lifted, but it just stayed. It stayed and like a fungus it grew, eating its way in, taking me with it one bite at a time.

Laying in bed night after night wondering what life was all about, sobbing, wishing I could disappear- I had a thought. What if I just did it? What if I just ended it? I was surprised I hadn't recoiled at it. I imagined how I would do it. I couldn't go on, I couldn't wake up another day, I couldn't take it anymore. I put it to the back of mind but there it was: an option I didn't have before. If I did do it, my mom would be the one to find me. Sobbing I realised I could never go through with it; I could never put my mother through that. That was my lowest point.

Although I stayed single throughout that time, intimacy was something that I still missed. I'm sure it contributed to my mental state, it was just another thing I couldn't get right after all. The man with the eyes kept popping into my head even though years had passed. Sometimes he was all I could think about and sometimes he would be forgotten for weeks, months. What was he doing right now? Was he happy? That time is a bit of a blur to me, I remember pieces.

I woke up one morning and I was enthusiastic. I felt motivated suddenly. It came out of the blue. I wanted to work, I wanted to get out and do something. I was eager to meet people... I started applying for jobs, all the while at the back of my mind thinking this feeling could disappear at any moment, and to try and make the most of it. I felt like a veil had been lifted. The darkness surrounding me had vapourised. I felt joy, happiness, and a zest for life that I hadn't felt in over 4 years. I was slowly coming back.

I got an interview almost straight away and was offered a job that I accepted. I loved it. I was happy for the first time in a long time. What was a chemical imbalance in my head had rebalanced itself somehow and my depression was dissolving away. I count ed myself lucky.

A few months into my new job and with my newfound confidence, I decided to give dating a go again. I signed up on an app and found myself excited at the prospect of connecting with someone. I swiped left and swiped right, giddy. I chatted with a few people. On my first date I met a man about my age, maybe a little older, who was a professor at a nearby university. We had hit it off on the chat and I was excited to meet him. I arrived at the café we had agreed on after work one evening and waited for him, cappuccino in front of me. I saw him arrive. I recognised him from his profile picture. He was shorter than I had imagined and wore a flamboyant paisley jacket. He reminded me of a peacock. He came over and we chatted, or should I say he chatted. He babbled on and on, droned on and on about himself, what he did, what he was working on , his childhood, his life, his likes and dislikes. Not one question about me. I left after that date, not so much disappointed but surprised, I hadn't met anyone so selfinvolved in a long time. I didn't see the peacock again.

The second time, I had been speaking to this guy who was about my age living in the next town over. We had been chatting for a while before we met up and when we did meet for drinks one night in a local bar, we hit it off. We chatted for ages and met again the following week. He told me that he was separated from his wife and had a young son, whom he saw on the weekends. No problem I thought, it's nice that he makes the time for his son. After a few dates and especially the ones that would bring us out in public, I noticed he was very fidgety when we would walk around. He wouldn't hold my hand in public. I asked him about it and he said he didn't want his ex-wife or any of their mutual friends to see him with another girl as it might upset her. After about a month or so we ended things mutually as I don't think we were what either of us was looking for. In hindsight I'm pretty sure he was still married and not technically separated as he had said.

As far as sex goes, he was ok. I can sum up the sex in all my relationships as: ok. There had never been any knee quivering, earth shattering experiences, at least not on my side. I hardly ever came and none of my previous lovers had ever willed themselves to do something about it. The intimacy of intercourse was something I always enjoyed at the start and it was enough for me, until it wasn't. When things got predictable and mechanical and they generally did eventually, I wondered if it was like that for everyone. I had accepted that I would always have to sacrifice personality for sexual compatibility and vice versa. Was it possible to have it all?

The man with the eyes, the fantasy. What would he be like in bed? Would we have had a connection sexually?

Chapter 3

The third date was with Lorenzo. We chatted for a few days before meeting at a cafe. He didn't have much English, but he was interesting to talk to and I enjoyed his company. At the end of our date, he asked if he could kiss me and I said "no, not yet!" I wasn't feeling it but met him again for dinner anyway.
 We met up a third time. I gave the kiss the go ahead at the end of the night and we found our groove. We stayed in the car kissing like two teenagers for over an hour. At one point there was a knock at the window and when I turned to see who it was there was a policeman looking in. I rolled down my window and he asked if I was all right, to which I chuckled and said yes sorry. He left and Lorenzo and I both laughed. When I got home that night I looked up at the sky and it was filled with stars. I've always loved a starry sky. I thought to myself, maybe things are looking up. Maybe the good evening spent, and the starry sky was a sign.

Gradually things got more serious and about 2 years in he moved in with me. Our sex life at the time was: ok. In the beginning I was reconnecting with having intimacy with another person and so I enjoyed that, and it was enough for me. After settling into a routine, intimacy took a blow and was at an all-time low. Everybody said it was normal for desire to plummet after years together, and I got that. But this was different somehow.
The man with the eyes .. I fantasised. I wondered if he remembered me .. what would I do if I saw him again? Would I approach him? Tell him who I was?
When I say Lorenzo and I's intimacy took a blow, I mean it was going to hit rock bottom anyway. It couldn't continue like it had been. We would make love, he would finish, clean himself up and then return to bed and fall asleep. Never was there any attempt to get me there, never any question even. That was just how it was. After a while I stopped letting him touch me, because what was the point? I wouldn't finish. We continued to have sex, but it was more so for him, because he wanted it. It was always shortlived. I tried talking to him about it, but nothing ever changed.

I would often fantasise about hot passionate sex with other men, sometimes just men I found attractive and sometimes the man with the eyes. Sometimes I became resentful that it was only fantasies and had to stay that way. Things with Lorenzo were impossible, and I explained to him that he was never concerned with my pleasure once he was done. It seemed to get through to him. I told him that I cared about him, which I did , and that I loved him , which I did , but that sometimes I felt as if I had to sacrifice my sex life to stay with him – or break up with him to save my sex life. He got it then I think- made more of an effort for a while but I had been so conditioned to recoil from any advances that it took me a lot of strength to open up again. I tried. I really did. But inevitably the old pattern returned.

I was still in my office job. The work was interesting, but I could never get used to the office environment. The claustrophobia, the toxicity when one or more people poisoned the group The sideways glances and hushed whispers, the stares and passive aggressivity. It was heavy. Thank God for my colleague Kat. She worked in the same team as me and she was German. When I first met her, she seemed a little stand offish, and I worried we wouldn't get along. It turned out she had such a sharp dry sense of humour, like me, and so we were as thick as thieves. We worked well, we laughed, we passed the time for each other. She was creative too like me.

Her true passion was pottery, and her desk was adorned with her unusual creations. Little pencil holders with boobs, little paperweights. One had a front like the head of a cat and the bottom like a cat's tail. I loved her designs.
She would often come in on Monday mornings and describe how she had spent the whole weekend working as she had had an idea for something, but it hadn't panned out the way she had wanted. I liked that she kept trying and always kept her work and displayed it proudly, no matter how unsatisfied she was with it. It was a part of her and of her journey, and that mattered to her almost as much as the end result.

I on the other hand never had the energy for my drawing. I loved it but could never motivate myself to start projects during the little time off I had. After three years at the office, Kat decided to leave. I was heartbroken. A friend of a friend of hers had gotten her an interview at another company, same kind of job, but for much more money. She was always broke despite our average salary, actually I was too. I couldn't blame her, more money is more money. She handed in in her notice and before I knew it her month was up, and she was gone.

We kept in touch and met up almost every weekend for drinks or coffee. She would regale me with tales from her new office, new gossip. Meanwhile I was stuck in the old office. I hated it know she was gone, I felt alone, and it was then I realised she had been the only person I actually liked there. There was talk of the company closing down and redundancies. I willed myself to hang on and wait it out until the end so that I could at least get some redundancy cash out of it. I hung on and hung on. I dragged myself there every day and dragged myself home every evening, my head aching, relieved another day was at an end, until eventually the last day came.

Once I was free, I decided to take a few months off before diving back in to another office job. The first few weeks I found it hard to relax and switch my brain off. After about 3 months, the deadline I had given myself, I still wasn't ready. I didn't have a choice I told myself, I had to work at some point. I couldn't afford to take so much time off. Just another couple of months was all I needed. That turned into another 6 months and during that time I was wracking my brain. What could I do instead of an office job? I was stuck. I didn't want to go back to my old life and wanted to do something new. Lorenzo started to get irritated. We fought. We fought all the time.

I was at an impasse and then, an idea! What if I started my own business? But doing what .. I liked to draw, maybe I could draw little postcards and have a little studio. Would people buy that? I had no money apart from the small amount I got when I left the company, but not enough to rent a studio or place. I would never qualify for a loan either. I spoke to Lorenzo one evening about it and told him my idea. I waited for his reaction.

"What do you think?" I said.
Silence. I couldn't read his face, but he didn't seem overjoyed.

"Yeeeeaaaah" he said, "but how would you sell your stuff?"

"Well, a studio maybe" I said, "maybe I can find a small studio in town, start small of course and also maybe sell them online "

"Yeeeahh" he said again, "where are you going to get the money though?"

"I don't know" I said, "that's the problem".

"Yeah" he said.

"Yeah" I said.

Ok, so not exactly a pillar of support there but then what am I expecting really. The reality is that I can't afford it. God, why does everything have to be so hard? How did regular people afford stuff like that? Businesses were opening left and right, how did average not rich people do stuff like that? I went to bed defeated. I had to think of something else to do or else start applying to office jobs . My eyes felt heavy, and I drifted to sleep. Tomorrow was a new day.

Chapter 4

The next day I was none the wiser. I started looking at job ads. Kat texted to ask if we were meeting. Oh, right it was Saturday today. I had been losing track of the days since I had been at home. I could have sworn it was Thursday, it felt like a Thursday, every day felt like a Thursday. Maybe she could help though. She was always straightforward and to the point. I liked that about her. People sometimes took it as rudeness when they didn't know her, but she never meant it that way. She would tell me what was what and set my head straight for sure. Let's meet for coffee in an hour, usual place? I texted back. She replied instantly with a thumb's up emoji.

I showered and got dressed. I put on my favourite boyfriend jeans (best invention ever, so glad the skinny jean fashion was dying down. I could never pull them off and ugh so tight!) and a warm jumper. I tied my hair into a loose bun and finally slapped on my lipstick. I couldn't go anywhere without my lipstick. I had two red and pink Chanel lipsticks.

They were precious to me, and I never left the house without one applied to my lips. My two Chanel lipsticks, my boyfriend jeans and my patent leather Doc Martin shoes, my three treasures. I threw on my coat and scarf and ran out. Our usual place was the local café Gola. We loved it there. It was right in the centre of the town on the main street. Inside, it was always warm and inviting with different couches, tables and chairs to choose from. It had an arty vibe to it with colourful abstract paintings on the walls. They were vibrant. Orange to yellow to blue, and the
side wall had a giant mural of flowers and leaves. The music was always great. It's probably why we had been attracted to it in the first place. We had been coming here for years. The best seat in the house was the one facing the big window. It was almost the length of the wall, facing out onto the main street. I loved watching people going about their day, watching the bustle, watching the towns heartbeat. Sometimes I would come alone and with my warm coffee and just sit still and observe.

Kat was already there and she had saved us the couch seat.

"Hey!" she said, "I ordered you your usual".

"Thanks, ugh I need it today" I said.

"What's up?" she asked "How's your job hunt going?

Lorenzo still on your case?"

"It's going, and yes" I replied rolling my eyes.

"Are you still looking at office job ads?" she said.

"Yeah, but look I wanted to get your advice on something"

I said.

"Okaaaay "she said hesitantly and laughed, "so serious! What's going on?"

I laughed. "No nothing serious but hear me out. You know how I don't want to go back to an office and hate nine to five right?" I started.

"Yeah, who does" she scoffed.

"And you know how I like to draw right?" I continued.

"Yeeeaaahhhh , where are you going with this ?" she said.

"Well what if , I set up a little studio and an online shop and just sell my drawings as little postcards and then make no money at all and end up homeless but at least I'm doing something I like so it's worth it ?" I said in one breath. I raised my eyebrows and grimaced and we both laughed.

"Okaaay "she said. She furrowed her brow. "I think that's a fantastic idea! "She exclaimed. "Where's your studio gonna be ?!"

"Okay so that's the problem right there, I have no money and can't rent a place" I said "What can I do? You think you know anyone that would give me a place right in a busy street but, like, for free?" I raised one eyebrow laughing.

"No" she said, "and if I did do you think I would be at my boring office right now?"

"True" I said, and our coffees arrived. I took off my coat and wrapped my hands around the cup, warm, a little shiver went up my spine. Kat took her phone out of her coat as she flung it on the back of the sofa and as she did her keys flew out and dropped on the seat.

"Oops your keys" I said, grabbing them.

"Oh, jeez thanks" she said, "my life would be over if I lost these. I literally have every key I've ever had on this holder". It was true, she had about 20 keys on there, it looked like something a janitor would have had for an apartment building. As I handed her the keys, I spotted her key holder. She had had the same one since I'd known her. A little dog made out of clay, one of her first attempts at an animal sculpture. It had three legs, and I wasn't sure if that was intentional, an occupational hazard, or if the leg had fallen off accidentally at some point during its lifetime. It had its three legs, two little spiky ears, a black nose and a short tail. It was orange with white spots. I loved it. It was the cutest thing I had ever seen, not despite but because of its imperfections. Suddenly I had a thought.
"Hey, wait a second" I said. I put down my coffee cup. "You're not happy with your job, are you?"

"No" she said, "of course not you know that".

"Why don't we do this together! "I said excitedly.

"Do what?" she said confused.

"Don't you see, its perfect!" I said hurriedly "Oh my god I can't believe I didn't think of this sooner! oh please say you'll do it with me oh it would be so much fun!"

"Wait, wait, what the hell are you talking about?" she said shaking her head.

"The business! A place!" I said "we could get a studio together! You make your ceramics and pottery and I make my postcards - we combine a space and sell together!"

Her eyes widened. "Oh my god what a fucking brilliant idea!" she said, "I could do my pottery and you your drawings, and we wouldn't sell anything cause were useless, but we'd be together!"

"Yes!" I said "this way we can both do something we like to do and hang on - can we really do this? "I asked, my face dropping.

"What do you mean?" she said buzzing from the new idea, "of course we can!"

"I know but I mean, can we afford it?" I said seriously, "do you think you could leave your job which pays well and rent a place with me knowing you may not make as much money, and all this could be a total bust?"

She thought about the question for a second. Finally, she said "look I love this idea, and I've always wanted to focus on my art. I have some money saved and not to sound impulsive here, but I think   it's totally doable. Would Lorenzo be ok with it?"

"Maybe not at first, I said, "but I mean if we're in it together it's not as risky as me doing it on my   own... I guess   I'll have to talk to him".
"Oh, fuck him" she said matter of factly and took a sip of her coffee. "You do what you fucking want to do and if you want to draw fucking postcards then we're gonna draw fucking postcards"

We both burst out laughing. She was always so chilled about things. Maybe it was because she was single, but she didn't answer to anyone but herself. I missed that sometimes, being single. She had been in a couple of semiserious relationships, but it had always gotten too much for her in the end. She was too independent and as soon as things got serious, she bailed. She was her own person and couldn't stand being stifled. I totally got that. With her blond hair and green eyes, she was no short of attention. She was curvaceous and loved her body, she was so confident, and it made her a magnet. She radiated beauty. She was a bit tomboyish in the way she dressed - dark jeans, black boots, band and skater t-shirts- but she made it look so feminine. I envied her. I wished I was as unapologetic about my b ody.

After a couple of hours of giddy babble, we parted ways.

"I'll txt you later" I said.

"Let me have a think and a look at the bank account" she said as she winked.

"Can't wait!" I said – "eeeeek so exciting!!" and with that we said goodbye and walked off in opposite directions.

Chapter 5

I walked home. I had nothing else on my agenda for the day and I didn't mind the walk. My house was right on the outskirts, about 30 minutes by feet. I was buzzing and my cheeks were flushed, the wind felt fresh on my skin. I was a genius, this was gonna be awesome. Is it socially acceptable for an adult woman to skip? I was floating on air. I wanted to start looking for a place straight away. I was so impatient; I would have rented a place tomorrow if I could. As I got closer to home, I thought of Lorenzo. What would he think? Would he be upset? It's not like he had to approve anything before I could decide. I could make my own decisions but if he wasn't happy, it would make things harder. Also, nobody likes killjoys.

"So, Kat is in on this with you?" Lorenzo said after I had filled him in on our plan.

"Yeah, well she's double checking her figures but she's into the idea for sure" I said.

"And she's gonna leave her job, her high paying job, to do what is it, boob pottery ? And you're both gonna make money from this?" he said quizzingly.

"Look she wants to leave her job, she likes making pottery, I like making my drawings, we want to at least give it a go" I said, "If it doesn't work out then it doesn't work out but at least we've tried".

"Ok...well good luck I guess" he said shrugging his shoulders.

"Thanks" I replied. "Plus imagine all the free booby jars you're gonna get". I wrapped my arms around him.

"Booby Jars ?!" he said laughing, "oh well now you've got me interested!". We kissed. I knew although he could be dismissive, he would support me .
It was hard to get to sleep that night, my mind racing with a million thoughts.

Kat texted me the next morning : I'm in, she wrote.
Woohooo!! I replied.
I had a look at some places we could   go
see – check these out she wrote back.
I clicked on the first link, and it was a retail space available to rent just on the edge of town. Not too big and not too small – woah but the price was high. I hadn't even thought about what the average going rate was. I guess it made sense for that type of space, especially close to town. The second link was for an even smaller space in the city centre, right near our favourite café. A great location, small, but we could make it work . Price was also high though. I replied : I'm free whenever you want.
In true German fashion , or Kat fashion , she dinged back 10 minutes later to say she had scheduled viewings for both   places   tomorrow   afternoon.
How she managed it on such short notice I don't know but she sure was efficient.

First viewing at 2 , m eet at the usual place at 1? s he wrote. See you then I replied.

Lorenzo had already left for work the next morning. He usually left around 6 in the morning, so I would rarely see him before he headed off. Weekends and weekdays, his schedule changed all the time. I didn't mind it as I liked having the mornings to myself. I liked the quiet. It's funny, in the beginning of our relationship I always pined for him as we didn't have much time free to spend together. I wished we could have had more mornings together to sleep in, to stay in bed. It seemed like so long ago. Now I savoured my time alone. I looked forward to it.

Since we were going to meet with agents today I decided to skip the boyfriend jeans and put on one of my favourite skirts, a calf length green skirt from one of my favourite brands, comfortable but cute. I loved skirts as much as boyfriend jeans. Today is a red day I thought choosing my lipstick. I slipped my docs on and I was out the door. I had savoured my alone time a little too much this morning and so I was running a little late. I checked my watch. If I hurried, I would be on time. I took off on the brisk walk to the town centre. It was windy, I hadn't noticed before I left. I found it a mystery that every time I wore either a dress or skirts, the weather turned out to be windy. It could be a totally calm day and as soon as the dress wenr on, BAM , windy , sometimes even gale force winds . The wind hit my face and made my eyes water. I clutched at my skirt as I walked to prevent it from blowing up and flashing the passing cars and poor passers-by. My hair was bellowing in

my face as I arrived, on time I might add to the café. Kat was already there, coffee waiting for me. She was the best. I sat down and took a breath.

"Oof , windy out there today!" I said, taking off my coat.
Kat cocked her head to the side and looked under the table.

"Skirt?" she said.

"Yeah skirt" I said, laughing as I rolled my eyes.

"So" she said, "what do you think of the places I sent you?"

"I think they're both good" I said, "although the price is slightly higher, I prefer the one closer to here in the centre. I think the more people pass it the better chance we have that they'll actually come inside and buy something!" "That's exactly what I think" she said nodding her head, "we're a new place, a new business, we need as many people as possible to be aware of us. If we're in a busy location we stand more of a chance not to go bust in the first week – it'll buy us a month at least" she smiled

I laughed, "a month!" I said, "You're more optimistic than I am!"

We discussed the price and per month we could each afford about 1000 which isn't huge to start with especially for a prime location, but we would see what we could find. As soon as we found a place she would give in her notice at her job, and she only needed to give one week so that was great, we wouldn't have to wait around and could get something as soon as it was available.

We went to visit the two places and they were nice, but they wouldn't work out. One was in a quiet location and the other one, the one we had been excited about, was actually way more expensive than we had thought. It was a no go. The agent who showed us the place, Amber, turned out to be the sister of an ex of Kats. They had become friendly at the time but had lost touch. She was so into our idea, she said she would keep her eye out for some cool spots for us.

We kept looking and after a couple of weeks Kat got a call from Amber. A space was being prepared for rent and she could show it to us before it went on the market officially. It was in the centre and right down the street from the café which was one of the busiest streets in town. We met with Amber one rainy evening to see it, and as she jingled the keys and pushed open the door with a thump, I felt it, the vibe, the good vibe. She turned on the light and there it was. A small room with brown brick wall, a concrete floor and a single solitary light bulb dangling from the ceiling. I loved it. It had so much potential. There was a large window looking out on to the street. I looked at Kat and knew she felt the same. Thanks to Amber the price was negotiable, and we decided there and then to take it.

We had done it! We were really doing it. Now we had to find equipment, tables for me, chairs and a workspace for me and Kat too. Displays and window displays, the list went on After that we had to figure out how to make it all fit.

Kat gave in her notice at work and sourced equipment while I went charity shop shopping for old tables, chairs and displays we could use. I ordered supplies, my fancy paper and some fancy pencils and brushes. I already had quite a collection at home, but I wanted some new tools for our new place. I already had a bunch of postcards I had drawn over the last few weeks and went to a local printer to have them printed onto fancy card.

We quickly got everything together and over the next two weeks our little snug started to come together. Kat had brought most of her tools from home, and we each brought frames to hang and decorative objects to pop around the place. Lorenzo helped us to hang some shelves, and a few potted plants later, we were done.

As you entered, Kat had her area and I mine in the form of desks, and we had placed display boxes and shelves all around so that people could browse. We had put together a display in the window too, my postcards and her clay figurines and jars. We added some twinkly lights and the place felt cosy. We had done it. Now for the official opening.

We advertised on social media as well as with the local radio stations and received quite a positive response. The local newspaper wanted to be there for our official opening so that they could feature us both in their paper and on their website. Thrilled with the advertising opportunity we accepted and before we knew it the day was upon us. We decided on the name "Bien Etre" studios. Bayer being her last name and LePretre being mine, we combined the two. Bien Etre also meant well-being. We both liked the ring it had. We had ordered a custom window sticker the length of the whole store front window and as soon as it arrived, we plastered it up. Seeing it up there for the first time made everything feel real.

The night before our grand opening I was so nervous, my mind racing. Had we checked and double checked everything? Were we doing the right thing? I couldn't stop thinking that this was my last shot and if this didn't work out, I would have to go back to a dull office job. It had to work.

Lying in bed curled up on my side, I closed my eyes and tried to quieten my mind. I felt Lorenzo turning in bed behind me and he placed his arms around me hugging me. He edged closer until his chest touched my back. I could feel his erect penis against me.
Not now, I thought, preoccupied with my first day jitters.
He cupped my breast and pressed his penis against me.

How long has it been? I thought. God, maybe 10 days? Let's do this, I guess. Inwardly I sighed. He pulled my underwear down until it reached my knees and staying in the same position, he adjusted himself so that he could enter me from behind. He did, slowly pushing deeper and deeper until he was fully inside me. I kept my eyes closed. I reached my hand behind me and placed it on his leg. He thrust once, twice, and then moved faster. A few more thrusts and he moaned as he pulled out, coming outside of me. He rolled onto his back, breathing heavily. A minute passed in silence. He lifted himself out of bed as he usually did and walked to the bathroom to clean up. He came back to bed.

 "Good night "he said, "love you".
"Love you too, good night" I said and drifted to sleep.

The next morning, I opened my eyes early. Lorenzo had already left for work. My alarm rang at 7 and I switched it off, already awake and thinking of big day ahead. The paper was coming to interview us, so I had to look nice. Ugh, I never look nice in photos I thought. I know it's a thing people say but for me it was the honest truth. I got a great kick out of people not believing me. They would snap a picture and their face would drop when they looked. "How is that possible?!" they would say. "You don't look anything like that in real life!". It was an affliction. Me and cameras didn't mix.

I got up and started making my coffee, checking my phone as it sputtered into the cup. A message from Kat flashed on the screen "Get ready it's the big day!! ". There was also an e-mail from Amber sent to both me and Kat wishing us good luck for the opening.

I drank my coffee and savoured the silence, the calm before the storm. I took a deep breath and sipped some more. Ok time to get dressed, I thought. What to wear? I picked out my blue knee length dress with the little sausage dog print, black tights and a mustard-coloured cardigan. I would add a nice belt to smarten it up maybe. I left my hair down. It had taken so long to grow back after I had cut it short. I had regretted it once the novelty wore off and vowed never to cut it short again. Now it came to just above my breast and I was leaving it that length. It had a mind of its own though, half wavy and half straight. Sometimes it looked great and other times all I could do was tie it up. It didn't look half bad today. Once dressed I applied some blush and a little bronzer to my face. I added some mascara. It's a red day today I thought as I painted my lips with my red lipstick. I grabbed my bag, my coat, put on my docs and I was ready to go. Checking my watch, I was on time. A message from Lorenzo pinged : good luck today! Love you. I messaged back :thanks love you too.

I headed out the door and started to make my way to our place. Bien Etre Creative Studios, I thought. I couldn't believe it was actually happening. As I approached the town, I could see the Saturday morning rush was beginning. I passed our favourite café and continued down the street. As I rounded the corner, I saw Kat already outside talking to a man and woman. They must be from the paper I thought. I got closer.

"Heeey!!" Kat yelled.

"Hey!" I said waving and smiling back.

"This is Kate and David from the paper" she said turning to the couple.

"Hi "I said, "nice to meet you, I'm Miriam".
"The other half" Kat said laughing.

The couple laughed and shaking my hand Kate said "nice to meet you".

"So big day!" David said.

"Yeah, for sure" I said and looked at Kat, "shall we open up?"

"Let's do it" she said.

She took the keys out of her coat pocket and unlocked the door. She opened it and flicked on the light as we all piled inside.

"Wow I love what you've done here, what a great space" Kate said. David took a camera out of his bag and fixed it around his neck. He held it up to his face and furrowed his brow as he squinted, aiming it at different objects around the room.

"Ok so I'm thinking I'll take a few shots of the inside here, and then we can do a shot of both of you girls standing in front of the shop window, sound good?" David said.

"Of course, "Kat and I replied

While David was busy snapping away, Kate asked us some questions about our work and what we would be doing here. We each talked about our own art and complemented each other's. When she was done, we went outside for our group photo. Oh no, I thought, here we go, try to at least look decent. Kat and I stood in front of the shop window right underneath our logo, with our arms around each other's shoulders as we posed for the photo.

"Big smile!" David said, and his camera clicked away. "Let's take a few more in case" he said as he continued snapping. I was trying to smile without looking too demented. Kat always looked good in photos so at least it wasn't all lost.

"Great, I think I've got it" he said, stuffing his camera back into his bag .

"Thanks so much" Kate said, "we wish you the best of luck! The article will be out next week but we'll send you both a quick message to let you know so you can keep an eye out for it" she smiled and we both waved as they walked away.

Kat and I looked at each other, and then turned to look at the shop.

"Ok" she said, "first order of business".

"Coffee" we both said in unison.

"I'll run down and grab some to go, back in a few minutes" she said.

I went inside and closed the glass door behind me. I looked around and took a deep breath. I sat down at my desk, my nice paper and fancy pencils waiting to be used . In that moment I was happy. What a great day, I thought .
Kat blew in minutes later, coffee in hand.
"Thanks" I said, taking the paper cup from her. We toasted and sipped our warm coffee, taking everything in. Finally she said, "ok let's get to work !" She sat at her desk and unwrapped some clay from her plastic clay bag. As she thumped a lump of it on the desk she said, "I think I'm gonna do a cow lamp ". I laughed, "sounds good" I said. I took out my first sheet of paper and my blue pencil and started my next ocean scene drawing.

Chapter 6

We had a few customers throughout the day. Most were just curious to see what kind of shop we had, but there was definitely some interest. We sold two postcards and a starfish mug. Success! I thought. We had lunch at the café and kept the shop open until about 6 that evening. What a fun first day, we both remarked. The next day was a Sunday and so we would stay closed, but it would give us time for our first day to sink in before starting a new week.

"See you Monday!" Kat said as we closed up that evening.

"See you Monday!" I said as we hugged. We walked away in separate directions.

That evening I told Lorenzo all about our first day and he was excited for us too. I was grateful he had been supportive, it meant I could really enjoy this.

We opened on Monday and by the end of the first week we had sold almost half of what we had brought in stock. It seemed that word of mouth was spreading, and more and more people came in to support us or to wish us luck and buy some of our work. I was relieved we were selling. I had been so afraid of not selling a thing and of being a complete failure. On Saturday morning we received a message from the newspaper as promised and Kat went out to the local shop to buy us a couple of copies.

She returned, newspapers in hand and slapped them on my desk. I took a one and she took the other. There, staring back at me from the front page was a large photo of myself and Kat.

"Front page?!" I said, shocked.

Kat looked amazing in the picture while I looked .. ok I guess. It wasn't the worst I had ever looked.

"You look great!" she said, "you were worried for nothing!"

"Yeah " I mumbled ." I wasn't expecting the front page though".

"It's on the website too!" Kat said tapping on her phone.

"Great!" I said, but really thinking oh god more photos of me out there. I cringed.

A couple of months passed, and we were doing well, keeping our heads above water, content with the decision we had made and loving being our own bosses.
One morning after a busy rush of customers we took lunch a little later than usual, at about 2. As soon as we would start gathering our stuff to leave, someone else would walk in and neither of us had the heart, or guts, to turn them away.

We finally made it to the café about 10 past 2 and the lunch rush was just starting to die down. The couch seat was taken of course, but Kat spotted a free table towards the back.

"I'll grab the table" she said, "you order?"
"Sure" I said as I made my way to the counter to join the short queue. I looked across at her. "TUNA SANDWICH?" I mouthed, and she nodded as she gave me a thumbs up. I advanced one spot in the queue and felt around in my pockets for change. I felt something in there I didn't recognise and pulled it out. An earring? Oh, that's right, I had taken these off on the way to work the other day as I had changed my mind about them mid walk. Where was the other one. I searched in my pockets again feeling my way around.

This was how I always lost earrings. My pockets were always a mess with cards, receipts and loose change. Ah, that must be it I thought, as I pinched a hard object in my other pocket, pinching with it some loose coins. Unable to single it out, I grabbed a fistful of my pocket ingredients. As I pulled my hand out to see if the earring was there, some coins and a couple of crumpled receipts dropped out and fell to the floor. They clanged on the tile and just at that moment the queue began to move again.

With only one person ahead of me, I bent down to gather my pitiful contents. I heard a man's voice "just a coffee please". Scooping up my rubbish, the earring among them I shoved everything back in my pocket, as I looked in front of me. I could see the back of the man's head. He had dark   hair and was taller than me. He paid and said thank you. I detected an accent and wondered where he was from. As he was about to turn around, a glint caught my eye on the floor. I looked down and saw a coin. It must be from my   po cket I thought and bent down to pick it up. When I straightened up the man was gone, and I stepped to the counter and placed my order. As I waited for the sandwiches and coffee to be prepared, I casually looked around the café, curious to see if the man had sat down. I didn't see him.

I took the tray and went to meet Kat at our table. "Oh good, I'm starving" she said as she grabbed her sandwich and took a massive bite.

"I know me too" I said and did the same with mine – a chicken salad sandwich.

We devoured our food in silence, both of us too hungry to talk. Afterwards we sipped our coffee and talked about the rest of the day ahead.

"Should we head back?" Kat said taking her coat from the back of the chair.

"Yep" I said, "just hang on a minute, I'm gonna use the bathroom really quick "

I got up and walked to the other side of the café, then down a small corridor leading to the back of the building. Once finished I washed up and walked back up the corridor. As I re-entered the café, my eyes looking at the floor as I walked, I wondered if the shop was going to be as busy this afternoon. Suddenly I felt a thump against my body. I had bumped into someone.

"Oh my god I'm so sorry!" I said as I reached my arm out, "I wasn't looking where I was walking". My eyes shot up to the persons face. I saw a blur of dark hair and loose curls. Our eyes met .

I felt my heart leap against my chest. I felt it almost leaping out of my body. A jolt. My brain scrambled to connect the dots. He stared back at me.

"Sorry" I blurted out. He paused.

"No problem" he said and smiled. He had a warm smile. I recognised the accent. It was the man I had seen earlier in the queue. Feeling embarrassed I started walking away. I was speechless. Could it be? I thought. No, it couldn't be. The man with the fucking eyes. That day years ago and those 60 seconds came flooding back to me. It was him. The hair, his eyes, his face. I remembered it like it was yesterday.

Reeling, my legs on autopilot, I arrived back to Kat at the table. I must have looked like I had seen a ghost because Kat asked me if everything was ok.

I turned my head and scanned the café. The man was making his way towards the exit. As he reached the door he turned, and our eyes met again. A second later he was gone.

"Well, what's up?" Kat said, "you're worrying me now !"
"Ok, oh my god" I said, "this is insane. Ok, I need to sit down. Ok, Jesus, this is crazy. Ok hear me out".

"Okaaay" she said tentatively.

"Do you remember that story I told you" I said, "about years ago when I met this guy on the street and-"

"And you both staaaared longingly into each other eyes" she said, "and your soooouls and your soooouls and it was deeeeeestiny-". She smiled as she rolled her eyes.

"Yeeees "I said," yeah him. Well, I just saw him".

"What?" she said, "what do you mean? Here?!"

"He just left, I said, "Oh Christ I need to calm down".

"Wait, are you sure it was him?" she said.

"Yeah definitely, I'm almost sure of it. I don't know if he recognised me or not though. He probably thought I was some kind of weirdo who was staring at him like a maniac after bumping into him" I said, putting my head in my hands.

"Like the first time then?" she joked.

" Yeah, like the first time" I laughed back.

"Well, he either knew who I was and didn't hang around, or he didn't know who I was. I don't know which is worse to be honest" I said.
All of a sudden, my high took a nosedive. I felt deflated. It was true. I mean if he didn't want to hang around then that was kind of shitty, and if he didn't even remember me then that was equally as shitty, wasn't it? I hadn't said anything to him either I guess. Maybe he was saying the same thing about me? I was shocked when I saw him and didn't know what to do, maybe it had been the same for him?

Still though what a crazy coincidence I thought, after all these years there he was in front of me again as if no time had passed, as if this was the most normal thing in the world to happen, so casual. It had all happened so fast. God I couldn't let myself obsess about this.

"Ok let's go" I said to Kat.

"Are you sure "she said? "You still seem pretty wound up".

"No, I'm alright I think" I said and smiled.

"Ok let's go" she said.

I grabbed my coat and scarf, and we headed out the door. Once I stepped outside into the cold air, it was like reality hit me in the face. Don't be stupid I thought, it was nothing. It had always been nothing. Things like this didn't happen in real life. I just had to push it to the back of my mind and not let myself get carried away in what was just a fantasy. Maybe it wasn't him after all.

We walked down the street back towards the shop. Kat kept saying how crazy this all was. For someone who didn't believe in destiny or fate or strange coincidences she was so giddy about the whole thing. We rounded the corner and as the shop blurred into view, I suddenly saw the outline of man outside it. I felt that jolt again. No, it couldn't be I thought. Probably just a customer waiting for us to open, or maybe a random person who just happened to be standing close to the shop.

As we got closer Kat said, "Who's that? Is that a customer waiting for the shop to open? God we can't even close for 30 bloody minutes" and she sighed heavily. My heart started beating faster and as we got closer I spotted his loose curls.

"I think that's him" I muttered to Kat under my breath.

"What?" she said.

"I think that's *him*" I said a little louder, still under my breath, trying not to look directly at him.

"The guy? that's him?!" she squealed loudly.

"Shhhhh yeaah" I said "will you keep it dowwwwn".

"Right sorry fuck ok be cool" she said.
As we got closer, he looked up. He looked at me, expressionless at first and then he smiled.

"Hi again" he said. He had a deep voice.

"Hi again" I said.

There he was right in front of me. His eyes, his beautiful eyes. His hair just as I'd remembered it, those curls, I noticed some grey, but it wasn't obvious. His beard and the shape of his mouth.

"Hi!" Kat said enthusiastically as she jingled the keys in the door before letting herself in. My heart was racing, and my insides felt as if they were melting. His smile. I had only ever seen it in my imagination.

"Sorry if this is awkward" he said laughing, "I mean, waiting for you like this".

"No, it's ok" I laughed. I tried to sound and look as casual as possible. Was this really happening? Something caught my eye, and it was Kat at the window behind him. I could see her moving her arms in the air, making big gestures, presumably to try to get me to laugh and loosen up.

"I think I know you" he said. When I heard those words, it felt like I had finally found a missing puzzle piece. He remembered me.

"I think I know you too" I said, trying to sound confident.

"Did we meet each other in Dublin, many many years ago?" he said. Oh god his voice, his accent, it was like a hypnotising melody. I tried to focus.

"I think we did" I said and automatically looked at the ground, blushing. Keep it together I thought. You're not 13, you've spoken to guys before.   I looked back at him, his gaze still on me.

"This is a bit crazy, no?" he said and laughed.

I laughed too. "It's completely crazy" I said.
"I'm glad you remember me at least" he said.

"I feel the same" I said- "are you from the area?".

"No" he replied, "I was just in the area for work actually. It's a complete coincidence I'm here too because my work is in the next town over, but I stopped off here for the day.
I'm from Italy, Palermo"

"Ah Italy" I said, "I've always wanted to go to Sicily, it looks so beautiful there".

"It is" he said and looked at the ground. He was still holding his coffee and he slid his other hand in his pocket. Without thinking, the next sentence out of my mouth was going to be about how Lorenzo was from Florence and so I had been to Italy many times. I stopped myself. I don't know why I did. It wasn't a secret. I didn't know this man I reasoned; he didn't need to know my life story.
 Lorenzo was Italian too, from Florence. I loved their traditions, his loud family. I had really fallen in love with the culture. We both loved our food and appreciated good food. Whenever we had a special occasion, we would spend hours planning what dishes we would prepare, even if it was just the two of us. Slow baked this and stewed that.

"Where are you from?" he asked.
"Well I'm French, but I've lived here for 15 years" I said. "Ah" he said, "France is also a very beautiful country, great food" – he smiled.

"That's for sure" I said and smiled back. That's for sure? I thought, you fool what are you blathering about.

"How did you know I was here?" I said motioning to the shop.

"Ah" he said, "it's not creepy I promise!" He laughed. "When I arrived yesterday, I was having a look around and I saw your photo hanging ins your shop window. I thought it was you but wasn't sure and so I wanted to stop by when you were open. You were closed when I did, so I went to the café for a quick coffee and when I saw you there, I knew it was you, but still came here to be sure".

"Oh ok" I said, "no not creepy! well I'm glad you did".

He smiled. I couldn't look away from him, God he was so handsome. Don't stare don't stare I told myself.

"What's your name?" he asked.

"Miriam" I said, "What's yours?".

"Francesco" he said.

We both smiled and shifted, it felt like we were both nervous.

"Would you like to have a drink with me? Or dinner?" he asked. My heart skipped a beat. Oh god yes.

"A drink would be nice!" I said.

"How about tonight?" he said, "Are you free?".
"Tonight, sounds good" I said.

"Why don't we exchange numbers, and we can message each other later?" he said.

"Ok great" I said and watched him take his phone out of his leather jacket pocket. He looked at his screen and I called out my number to him. He tapped it in and then looked back at me. My phone rang. I took it out of my coat pocket and saw a number I didn't recognise flashing on the screen.

"Now you have mine" he said.

"Ok cool" I said.

"Ok well I'll let you get back to your work" he said smiling.

"I'll talk to you later" I said.

We both hesitated, smiled, and then turned to walk away slowly. We both looked back at each other. Embarrassing! I thought. I was floating on air though. I floated into the shop and shut the door. I stared at Kat.

"Well??" she said excitedly.

"Well, it's definitely him" I replied.

"Unbelievable" she said, "so what now?"

"He invited me out for drinks later" I said blushing.

"You're going right?" she said.

"I think so" I said smiling. I was still in shock.

"At least you know now that he felt the same as you all that time" she said.

"I guess" I said. It was   true, I did feel relieved . It hadn't all been in my head after all. I needed to think, I needed to calm myself down.

Francesco. I had never really thought about what his name was. He was just a face. Now he had name and a heavy presence. He was real.

Chapter 7

The rest of that afternoon was a blur. I couldn't concentrate. I checked my phone every 5 minutes in case he messaged. Would I have to message first? I didn't want to seem eager. Around 6 as we were closing the shop, my phone pinged. Nervously I turned on the screen and saw an unread message from Francesco. I had been so tempted to save his number under "the man with the eyes", I couldn't get used to the idea that he had a real name. I opened the message:

Hi Miriam, it's Francesco from earlier, are you still ok to meet up for a drink?

"It's him" I said to Kat, turning red.

"Well," she said, "reply! But please text me later and let me know where you're meeting and at what time. He is a stranger after all, and you can't be too careful"
"I will" I said.

"Will you tell Lorenzo?" she asked.

Lorenzo, oh god Lorenzo. I would tell him, there was nothing to hide. It was an exceptional circumstance after all, and there was nothing romantic here, nothing sexual. I had forgotten he was going for drinks after work with his work friends and he wouldn't be home until late. I'll message him when I get home I thought.

"Yeah, I'll tell him, nothing to hide right?" I said.

"Right" she said.

"Ok talk to you later" she said, "and message me !!"

 "I will!" I said. We hugged. I started walking home. It was the first time all day I could be alone with my thoughts. Was I really meeting him now? Tonight? I messaged Francesco back:

Hi, sure! , do you want to meet at Stoney's bar at around 8 ? I hit send. I felt a wave of anxiety rising in me. This morning everything had been normal and now my world had been turned upside down. When I arrived home, I messaged Lorenzo:

Hey, just to let you know I'll be going for drinks this evening with an old friend, long story. I'll talk to you about it tomorrow. Have a great night! I might see you when you get in tonight. Love you. I wrote.

I would keep it short and explain it to him properly when I saw him tomorrow. It was 6.30 so I had about an hour to get ready, more than enough time. Or so I thought. What was I even going to wear? I hopped into the shower. As I finished and wrapped myself in a towel, my phone pinged. Having kept it close by on the sink I checked it straight
away. It was from Francesco.

That's perfect I'll see you then! it read.

What was I going to wear? Ok I was meeting someone but it wasn't a date. I was with someone and he probably was too for all I knew. I had to stay casual. Still, I wanted to look nice. I picked out a red skirt – mm, would red give him the wrong idea? I didn't want to take the chance. I discarded it onto the pile of clothes that was forming on my bed. After trying almost everything on and trying to make my outfit scream "I'm casual and this is not a date", I settled on my calf length cream satin pleated skirt and my loose navy jumper. I left my hair down. I had had it tied up in a bun all day and it was a bit messy, but it would pass. I applied some blusher and bronzer to my face and some light mascara. I wanted to go for my red lipstick but thought it might be too... datey. I went with the pink one. For earrings I couldn't make up my mind .. and then I remembered the ones in my coat pocket. I fetched them and tried them on. They would do. They were understated, short pendants with a turquoise bead,   just a pop of colour. Plus, they matched my eyes.
I glanced at the time as I strapped my watch back on my wrist. It read 7.20. I had to leave soon. Then the sweating began. What am I doing? I thought I must be out of my mind. I was going for drinks with a random stranger that I met for a few seconds over a decade ago. Still, I wasn't going to miss this. He remembered me.
A few last finishing touches and I headed out. It would take me about 30 mins to get there. The walk would calm my nerves. En route I messaged Kat : Hey just on my way to Stoney's bar x There was a reply from Lorenzo: H   ey ok have fun talk to you tomorrow love you.
Ok I thought, this was it. I didn't know what to expect. I mentally prepared myself to meet someone that was completely different to what I had imagined him to be for all these years. I prepared myself for a let-down. Surely there was a catch. I was sure there would be a disappointment of some sort. Maybe he wouldn't even show up at all.

As I got closer to the bar, I could feel my heart in my mouth and a ringing in my ears. I hadn't been this nervous in years. It was almost thrilling.
I checked my watch. 7.55. I would arrive just on time. The streets were alive. It was dark already, but the bar and restaurant lights twinkled brightly. It was Friday night and there was a buzz in the air. I could hear people laughing in the distance and the loud hum of merry chatter. I saw the bar ahead of me. There was a group of people outside and I couldn't see if Francesco was there. I would wait outside for him if he wasn't. I stepped past the group all the while scanning the street, and suddenly there he was.
He turned and as he saw me, he smiled and waved. I waved back and smiled too. God that smile I thought.

"Hey!" I said.

"Hey" he said, "nice to see you!".

"Yeah, its been a while" I said laughing.

"True" he said and chuckled.

"Should we go inside?" I said

"After you" he said, and I stepped in to the bar. I spotted a small booth towards the end of the bar and turned to Francesco and pointed to it.

"Is there ok?" I asked.

"Perfect" he said. We sat down and I took off my coat.

"Drink?" he said.

"Yes please, mmmm , not sure what to get, ammm a beer please a Heineken" I said.

"Ok be right back" he said. I watched him walk to the bar and lean on the counter.
He looked nice. He was well dressed. He had on dark blue jeans that weren't tight or baggy, just well fitted, and a dark navy fine knit wool jumper . As he sat back down with our drinks, two Heinekens, I noticed he smelled of
soap, he was freshly showered. It smelled delicious.

"So" he said lifting up his glass, "cheers!"

"Cheers" I said raising my glass and clinking it against his. Our eyes met and as we moved the glasses to our lips, we didn't break our gaze. His eyes were so intense. I was surprised at how well I had remembered them after all these years. That feeling I got the first time we had met, it was the same now, the same feeling of comfort. It felt like I knew him. I took a sip and put my glass down.

We talked about ourselves and of that day in Dublin. He was a freelance street photographer and at the time he was just starting out. Ireland had been one of his first travel assignments and when we met it was on his last day here. He had flown back home the next morning. He said he had regretted not saying anything in the moment. I told him I did as well. It was as if we were old friends. The conversation flowed.

He was funny and I liked that we shared the same sarcastic sense of humour. There was a connection, and that was something I had always wondered if we would have. As we drank and talked the time melted away and I felt like we were the only two people in the world. There was a spark. When the topic moved to relationships, I felt my bubble suddenly burst. I had been so engrossed in him that Lorenzo hadn't even entered my mind. I couldn't not tell him about Lorenzo, but I didn't want to. I wanted to stay in this bubble. He said he was single, but he had come out of a long-term relationship recently. and the break-up had been hard on him and her. They had been together about 10 years but had never married or had children. Weirdly and perhaps unfairly I felt relieved at that. He asked about me and I told him about Lorenzo. That we lived together here, not married and no children. He looked down into his drink.

We changed the subject and carried on talking, my bubble reforming itself. The bar was closing soon. I checked my watch, and it was almost 1. That went by so quickly, I wished we had more time I thought. I didn't want it to end so soon. He was leaving town in a couple of days he said. I was too afraid of sounding eager, so even though I wanted to immediately ask him to do something again the next night, I stopped myself. As we left the bar we hovered in the street. I said I was going to catch a taxi home and he said his hotel was only a few minutes' walk away, so would wait for the taxi with me. It was cold, I was tipsy and high from the evening, high from him. Secretly I hoped a taxi wouldn't come for ages, but of course one came almost straight away.

"Well," I said, "this was nice, it was so great to meet you finally".

"Same here" he said, "let's keep in touch".

"Definitely" I said and smiled.

He leaned in to kiss my cheeks goodbye. I felt his beard on my skin and the warmth of his face, and as he kissed my other cheek, I breathed him in. He smelled of home. All I wanted in that moment was to feel his lips on mine.

"Bye" he said "have a good night".

"You too thanks again" I said and climbed into the taxi. As it drove away, I looked out the window. He was gone. I got home and Lorenzo wasn't back yet. I was relieved. I needed to be alone. I replayed the night over and over again in mind as I changed for bed.

It had started to rain, and I could hear it against the house. As I lay in bed I stared out of the window in the ceiling at the stars and listened to the rain pattering against it. Now I could properly think. I loved looking at the stars. When we were looking for a place to move to, I chose this house mainly because of the large Velux window in the ceiling in the bedroom. I moved the bed underneath it as soon as we moved in. Lorenzo hated it, complaining it was too bright and it would bother him. I didn't care. It was my one condition, my one thing. How comforting it was laying there under a carpet of stars. Some twinkling brightly, others dipping in and out of focus. That's the real magic. A whole universe brimming with mysteries waiting to be discovered, solved. Sometimes it overwhelmed me. How can people go about their everyday life when there's a whole dimension up therewe don't understand
        – it fascinated me. So, I looked at the stars. The rain, the wind picking up outside. I loved it. As I listened my eyes felt heavy, and feeling myself drifting off I gave in, blanketing the chaos in my mind and falling to sleep.

The next morning, I woke up at the usual time, 7. Lorenzo was asleep in bed next to me. That's right, he had a day off today, I had forgotten. I hadn't heard him come in last night. I tiptoed out of the room so as not to wake him and made my way down the hall to the kitchen. Fresh coffee in hand, I stared into nothingness as I sipped and thought of last night. He hadn't asked to see me again. I felt disappointed. Maybe it was for the best. I did have feelings for him, whatever they were, and it wasn't a good idea to push things. I heard Lorenzo stirring. He shuffled down the hall and walked into the kitchen.

"Hey" he said with a raspy voice.

"Hey I didn't hear you come in last night, good night?" I said.

"Yeah, we had one too many, I think I got back around 3 in the morning" he said.

"You must be tired" I said.

"I'm ok" he said, "just need coffee".

"So, what's your plan for today?" I said.

"I think I'm just gonna take it easy at home" he said, burying his head in his hands.

"Listen" I started – now is as good a time as any. He looked up.

"So, the craziest thing happened yesterday" I said, "so I never told you this, but you know years ago when I lived in Dublin?"

"Mmmmhmm" he said taking a sip of his coffee.

"Well, so while I was there, I had this weird thing happen one day in the street" I said. He looked at me and went pale. His face was as white as a sheet.

"So, I met this guy on the street one day" I continued, "and it was a bit weird cause we didn't speak to each other, we just kind of looked at each other" God it sounded so ridiculous when I said it out loud.

"Oh god" he said.

"Oh no it's not what you think" I said.

He slapped his hand to his mouth and held it there as he started running towards the bathroom, where he proceeded to empty the contents of his liquid breakfast into the toilet. Maybe I'll tell him another time I thought. I went to get dressed and used our other bathroom. When I was done, I poked my head round the main bathroom door to find him hugging the toilet bowl.

"Are you ok?" I said. Stupid question really.

"I feel like shit" he said as he retched.

"Fuck, sorry" I said, "do you need anything? I have to head into work, but I can bring something by here at lunch if you want?"

"No, I think I'll be ok" he said. I stepped inside and stroked his head.
"Poor baby" I said," I wish there was something I could do to help".

"It's alright" he said, "I'll get into bed and text you when I wake up".

"Ok" I said, "I'll talk to you later, love you".

"Love you "he said.

As I left the house, I could hear him retching from the bathroom- poor thing I thought. I'll come by at lunch anyway and bring him something to eat.

I arrived at the shop and Kat was already inside unwrapping her previous days ongoing work. It looked like a lump with tentacles. I didn't ask.

"Heyy" she greeted me excitedly as I walked in.

"Hey!" I said and walked to my desk.

"So?" she said, "How was it??"

"Well Lorenzo's sick and he's been projectile vomiting all over the apartment since this morning" I replied.

"I meant how did it go with Frrrancesco" she said and she rolled the R in Francesco dramatically, "but Lorenzo's vomiting? is he ok ? ah wasn't he out last night with the guys ?!"

"He was" I said rolling my eyes.

"Aaah ok I'm not worried then" she laughed, "I'm sure he'll live".

"I feel sorry for him though" I said, "I might go see him during lunch just to drop   something off for him to eat".

"Aww" she said, "you guys are such a cute couple". I felt a pang of guilt. "So, out with it how did it go last night ??"

I smiled and got my pencils out. "Ok, I could swoon" I said "Do people still swoon? . He made the whole situation feel completely comfortable. Turns out he's a photographer and he's just so nice honestly, we talked all night, it flew by".

"Wow that's great" she said, "I was worried he would turn out to be a dick and it would upset you".

"I'm relieved too if I'm being honest" I said.

"So is he in town for long" she asked.

"For another couple of days, and before you ask, we haven't made plans to see each other again" I said.

"Uh oh" she said, "are you ok with that?" She knew me so well.

"Yeah!" I said, "of course!"

She raised her eyebrows as if to say *yeah right*. The morning was quite busy with lots of customers popping in and out. At lunch time I went to the café to get a sandwich for Lorenzo. I walked home and as I let myself in, I heard the tv on in the sitting room. He was out of bed anyway that was good, I thought. He was laying on the couch.

"How are you feeling?" I said.

"Hi, I'm a little better" he croaked.

"Have you had anything to eat?" I asked.

"No not yet" he said.

I handed him the sandwich. "BLT" I said.

"You're the best" he said as he sat up and took it from me. I smiled. I had brought my own sandwich so that we could eat together. We ate, and I thought of telling him about Francesco. Now didn't feel right. Plus, Francesco was leaving soon, and we wouldn't see each other again, so there wasn't any urgency really. I'll wait until he's feeling himself again to tell him, I thought. We finished our sandwiches, and I made him a coffee and brought it to him on the couch. I kissed him goodbye.

"Talk to you later ", I said.

"Love you" he said, "thanks for the lunch". I made my way back to the shop.

I really did love Lorenzo. He was so caring, and he was a genuinely nice person. You don't find people like that too often. I was really lucky. He was kind too, a trait that's also not too common. People are often kind on the outside, but you quickly see that's not who they really are. He was truly kind. I needed that in a partner. As I arrived back to the shop my phone pinged. Probably Lorenzo, I thought. I turned on the screen. It was Francesco.

My heart leapt. I quickly opened it and read: Hi Miriam, it was so great to see you last night. Since I'm still in town for a couple of days would you like to get together again?
Maybe for dinner tonight if you're free?

I sat down. Kat was busy with a customer. I put the phone down and picked up my pencil. I started colouring in the card I had been working on, on autopilot. He wants to meet again, I thought. Tonight. God, he doesn't waste time. I liked that, he wanted to see *me*. I wanted to see him too. I was scared though, scared of my feelings becoming more intense. I didn't want to jeopardise my relationship with Lorenzo. I knew how quickly I could get swept up and how I could read too much into things. I didn't know what to do. I reasoned with myself. What's the harm? He knows I have a boyfriend; he knows it's a serious relationship. What could really happen? It's not a date. He's asking me to dinner because he also enjoys my company. It could be the start of a great friendship, couldn't it? I'm going to do it, I thought. Would he find it strange that I was available all the time though? He's not giving me much notice; would it be weird? Fuck it. I picked up my phone and hit reply: Hey Francesco, sure that sounds good. Do you have a place in mind? I hit send.

I was excited. I had to tell Lorenzo now. He was at home this evening so I would tell him when I got home. Would he

approve of dinner with another man?

I would figure it out.

My phone pinged again, and it was Francesco. It said: I read that the restaurant "Apple Orchard" is   good, should we meet there at 8?

I had heard of it but had never   been, it was on the other side of town. Not fancy fancy but still a nice place. I replied:
Sounds great see you then.

I told Kat my news once she finished up with her customer. She was excited, but she did say a dinner felt a bit datey. I told her he knew I was in a relationship, and she said that as long as he knew it wasn't a date and that I told Lorenzo, there was no harm. That it would be good for us to have a friendship out of this.

We closed up at the end of the day and she wished me luck for that evening. Once I got home, I found Lorenzo in the same place on the couch. To be honest I was glad he was relaxing. He didn't have much time off from his job and when he did, he always tried to get as much done as possible. He never just sat down and took it easy, and he needed it.

"How are you feeling" I asked.

"Much better thanks" he said. I sat down beside him and kissed him.

"I was thinking pasta for dinner" he said.

"You always think pasta for dinner" I laughed.

He laughed back and said, "yeah but I was thinking a reeeally nice pasta, what do you think?"

"Actually …" I said, "I might be going out for dinner this evening .."

"Going out AGAIN" he laughed, "that's not like you !"

"I know I know" I said.

"Going with Kat?" he asked.

"No actually, I've been wanting to tell you, it's a funny story" I started.

"Oh, go on" he said.

"Right, well, do you remember a few years ago before you and I met I lived in Dublin?" I said.

"Yeeeaaahh" he said squinting as if trying to remember.

"Well so when I was there - this is gonna sound mental – so when I was there I had a weird thing happen where I met this guy but we didn't talk and we just had a weird moment. It was bizarre and I never saw him again" I blurted.

"Okaaaay" he said. He looked confused and I didn't blame him.

"Right, well its crazy, see, I bumped into him yesterday and we both remembered each other, isn't that mad?" I said.

"Yeah, that's a bit, I mean, I don't know what that is" he said.

"Right, well anyways I went for a drink with him last night to catch up" I said.

"Catch up?" he said, "catch up on what? I thought you said you didn't know each other?"

"Well, yeah ok, not catch up but I suppose it's such a weird situation it was just to kind of talk about it, and you know become friends I suppose" I said

"Right" he said, "so is what you're telling me that you're now going out for dinner with this guy?"

"Yeah, that's what I'm saying" I said, "look, he's from Palermo, he doesn't live here and he's only here for a couple of days before he leaves. That's why we're meeting again, it's just because of the limited time he has. It's a friendly dinner, that's all, and I won't be back late".

Lorenzo looked pissed.
"Ok" he said, "well I can't tell you what to do, you can do what you like, but I'm not happy about it".

"I know you're not, I can see that" I said, "but it's just friendly I promise".

"Hmmm "he said. He got up and went to the kitchen. Banging the pots and pans and slamming the cupboard doors, "Pasta for one then I guess" he said.

"Oh, don't be like that" I said and walked over to him. I put my arms around him from the back and hugged him. "You know I love you" I said. He didn't answer.

"Cmon, I'll try to get back early, and we can have a cuddle, would you like that?" I said.

"Hmmm" he said. He turned to face me. I kissed him and he smiled.

"Ok, I'll hold you to that" he said. I smiled.

"I'd better go get ready" I said, and his face fell for a second. "Back in a minute" I said and went to go take a shower.

God that was awkward, I thought. I didn't feel right dressing up too much, not in front of Lorenzo. I didn't want him to worry him even more. I wasn't sure what to wear, it was a nice restaurant so I couldn't be too casual. I opted for my knee length yellow tartan dungaree skirt and a loose v neck jumper underneath. I tied my hair up in a loose bun and applied some makeup and my pink lipstick. I added some nice earrings, black tights underneath my skirt and my docs. Perfect, dressy but relaxed.

When I walked out of the bathroom Lorenzo glanced sideways at me, trying to look without making it obvious. "Oooohhhh fancy" he said mockingly.

"It's not fancy what are you talking about" I snapped.

"Hmmmm" he said.

"I'd better go" I said, and went to kiss him. "I'll talk to you when I get back".

"Hmmm" he said again, "and where are you going?"

"To the Apple Orchard" I said.

"Ooohhh fancyyyy" he said in a high-pitched voice. I laughed – "Shut up" I said and kissed him again.
"See you later".

I walked out the door and checked my watch – 7.35, oops I was running a bit late. I started the brisk walk and halfway in it started to rain. Oh, fuck's sake I thought. I saw a taxi and decided to flag it down. If I walked the whole way in this, I would be soaking wet. The taxi picked me up and 10 minutes later we pulled up to the restaurant. I paid him and as I opened the door to get out, I looked up, and there was Francesco, standing outside the front door of the restaurant under its shelter. I smiled and waved, and he did the same. I could feel my heart pounding against my chest and tried not to give my nervousness away.

"Hi! crazy weather!" I said as I got close to him.

"Hi! I know! It came out of the blue too!" he said.

Suddenly he leaned in to kiss me hello. He smelled amazingly good. I let the scent wash over me.
His soft beard brushed against my cheek. I felt a jolt go through me as it did. Get it together I told myself. We went inside and as our table wasn't ready yet, they suggested we wait for a few minutes at the bar. The place was crowded. There were so many people, it was crammed tonight. We edged our way through the crowd and finally reached the bar, both leaning on the countertop. We ordered our drinks as the crowd behind us tightly squeezed us in. Suddenly there was some jostling and I felt myself being pushed as my body squashed itself against Francesco's.

"Oops sorry" I said laughing and he laughed too.

"They're a bit wild tonight" he said smiling.

I could feel his body against mine. It felt strong. He looked down at me and I looked up at him. His eyes, his expression had changed. His eyes were wide. I looked away and peeled myself from him. I felt my cheeks flush. My face felt hot. I stared down at my drink. I took a sip. The energy I was feeling, the attraction I was feeling, it was there. I knew it was wrong. I couldn't help it.

Our table was soon ready. We sat down and I felt a buzz, an excitement. We picked up where we had left off the night before and the conversation flowed once more. We talked and talked, and I lost track of time. Before we knew it, they were closing. I had had a couple of drinks and was feeling tipsy. We left the restaurant and Francesco suggested we go for a last drink, there was bar down the road. I agreed, not wanting to leave and secretly relieved he had suggested it.

We continued our conversation in the bar and soon they were closing too. We had been sitting beside each other and the more we drank the closer we inched together.

We were enjoying each other so much that it felt natural. When the night was over, we found ourselves on the street again waiting for a taxi. Would I mind if we shared this one, he asked, as his hotel was a bit further away this time. I didn't mind at all. A taxi stopped for us, and I climbed in first. He followed and closed the door behind him. It was dark. As the car moved off, our knees suddenly touched briefly. I felt as if lightning had struck through me.

We arrived at his hotel first.

"Thanks for a great night" he said. He placed his hand on my knee and squeezed. I felt the electricity once more. He leaned in to kiss my cheeks goodbye. The combination of it all made me weak. The darkness, my head fuzzy from the drinks, his hand on my knee. His scent enveloped me, his beard against my skin , his warmth . It took everything I
had in that moment to not move my lips to his. But I didn't.

"Bye "I said quietly, "I had a great time".

"Talk soon" he said and got out.

"Talk soon" I said. As the taxi pulled away, I stared ahead as slowly my heart rate returned to normal.

On the journey home I felt elated. Arriving home, my heart sank. I paid the driver and went inside. Please let Lorenzo be asleep, I thought. I walked inside and heard the TV. Entering the sitting room, I saw Lorenzo asleep on the couch. I turned off the TV and the lights and got ready for bed. I thought about Francesco and what my feelings for him meant. What it meant for me and Lorenzo. I felt guilty. I had never cheated on anybody in my life. I had it done to me though , and when I found out about it afterwards I remembered feeling so angry , but also so embarrassed that
it had been going on behind my back for so long.

It had gone on for months, and during that time his friends and everybody knew. I remembered the get togethers we had had with these friends and how they had acted completely normal. I couldn't wrap my head around how someone I thought I knew, someone I was sharing my life with, was doing this and then coming home to me continuing the charade. To what end? I felt resentful that my time had been wasted. I wouldn't wish it on anyone. I didn't feel like I related to that. I cared for Lorenzo.

Yes, I had developed feelings for someone else, but I hadn't acted on them. I couldn't control how I felt, I could only control my actions and choices. Francesco was leaving anyway, and I wasn't sure if we would see each other again. If we did, I wasn't going to throw my entire relationship and my life away for what? A kiss? I wanted him though, I felt connected to him. I was torn. I pictured it happening, the kiss, and then the secret, the guilt, the lies. Could I carry on without telling Lorenzo? I wouldn't cope with such a heavy conscience; I knew I wouldn't.

Chapter 8

The next morning when I woke up Lorenzo had already left for work. I had the day to myself and looked forward to chilling out. I drank my coffee and poured myself a bath. As I got in, I felt the hot water soften my muscles and I relaxed. I slid deeper inside and closed my eyes. Why now I thought, why all this now? I had my life together, I was with a great guy, had a nice house and a job I liked. Everything had finally come together. Then this happened and now I was questioning everything. I stopped myself.

I let my thoughts drift to work, to the shop, to Lorenzo. Suddenly my phone pinged. My eyes sprang open, was it him? I bent over the bath to grab my phone laying on the floor and turned it on. Message from Francesco. I took a deep breath and read it:

Hi Miriam, last night was great. I'm leaving today, in the late afternoon, could we meet for a quick coffee before I go?

I shut the phone off and sank back into the bath. To meet him one last time, I thought. It would just be a coffee, in a public place, in the daytime. I doubted my feelings would be so uncontrollable in a setting like that. I could easily trust myself. I thought about being too eager and always free for him. I thought some more and finished my bath. When I got out, I replied:
I think that should be ok, I have a couple of hours free in the afternoon if you like around 1? We can meet at the café.

I looked at myself in the mirror and Lorenzo's things caught my eye. His deodorant bottle, his toothbrush, his towel hanging on the wall . What was I doing I thought.
He replied: Great see you then!
I got dressed and stayed causal in jeans and a loose jumper. I tied my hair in a loose bun and slipped on my docs. It was 12 and so I decided to head out early. I needed a coffee.

When I arrived, I took the free couch facing the window and ordered a large flat white. I flicked through someone's discarded newspaper while I waited. I checked the street outside constantly and sometime later I saw him. He looked through the window as he passed by, and I waved. He caught my eye, smiled and waved and came inside.

"I'll just order a coffee" he said. I nodded as he made his way up to counter. He bought his coffee and sat down beside me on the couch. I felt good now he was here.

"So, you're heading out today?" I said.

"Yes" he said, "I'm driving to Connemara to take some photos and then heading back to Dublin in the afternoon. I have my flight tomorrow night to go back to Italy".

"Ah you must be happy to be getting back home", I said.

He shrugged. "I guess", he said, "but it's nice here, I wish I had more time to explore it". He looked at me and smiled. I returned his smile and looked away. I could feel myself blushing.

"Maybe one day I'll see you in Italy?" he said, "You're always welcome to call, I can show you around".

Maybe one day, I repeated his words in my head. It was really all over. But what did I expect? A proposal? Of course he was going back home to his life, we didn't know each other, we were strangers.

"Oh, for sure!" I said, "and you too if you ever come back here to.. explore".

"Of course," he said smiling. We sipped our coffees. The atmosphere between us felt different today. There was a hesitation that hadn't been there before. We chitchatted; it was light conversation. He finished his coffee and suddenly slapped his hands against his thighs.

"Well," he said, "I'd better go". Go? I thought, we had only been sitting down for 20 minutes and he wasn't even leaving town until late afternoon.

Disappointed I said, "Oh! Ok then!", trying not to sound hurt. We both stood up and he grabbed his coat.

"It was great to have met you again, and to have spent this time with you" he said. He quickly kissed my cheeks. It had all happened so fast.

"Likewise," I said, "let's stay in touch".

"Of course" he said.

"Safe trip, safe drive" I said.

He put his hand on my arm. "Thanks and have a good day, talk soon ok ?".

"Talk soon" I said, and he walked out.
I watched him through the window as he disappeared out of my sight. I could feel my eyes welling up. That was it. It was done. That's was it? Why had he been so cold? What had changed? He was gone and apparently our spark was something I'd imagined. I had been so naïve. I hated that I was so naïve sometimes, always hoping for something more .
I sat back down on the couch and continued staring out the window for a few moments. I fought the tears back. I had to leave now I thought, I needed to get home. I would have a cry there, get it all out and then carry on with my life . It was probably for the best that it had ended so abruptly anyway, this way I could stop feeling guilty for the feelings I was having for him.

Trying not to burst into tears I grabbed my coat and walked quickly out the door. I started to make my way down the street and couldn't hold it back any longer. I bowed my head and felt warm tears trickling down my face. I wiped them away angrily. Stop being so stupid, I thought. He had done nothing wrong. I knew that but I just needed to be sad. Sad that I had felt desired for the first time in years, and it might not have even been desire after all. Of course, he hadn't desired me. Fuck, I'm an idiot. I remembered that night in Dublin when I had walked down that cobbled street alone, feeling like a fool, like a fool who thought incredible things could happen to her and they never did. That's how I felt now. I had come so far since then, yet here I was. I was the same fool.

My face felt hot and wet. I went to bury it in my scarf when I realised, I didn't have it on. I stopped – fuck I had left it in the café. I briefly thought about not going back and just leaving it there but turned around anyway and headed back. My head still bowed, my pace was brisk. I just wanted to get out of here, to get back home and close the door behind me, to let the tears engulf me, to feel sorry for myself. I stepped into the café and spotted my scarf still on the couch. I grabbed it and wound it around my neck, burying half my face into it. I didn't want to be seen. More tears flowed quietly. Back on the street and eyes on the pavement, I had walked a few steps and was quickening my pace.

Suddenly I felt my body pound against something. I had bumped into someone. Not wanting them to see my face, I muttered "sorry". I glanced up and felt a jolt.
Francesco.
Embarrassed, I tried not to make eye contact.

"Oh hey" I said, trying to make my voice sound as cheerful as possible. He didn't answer. I glanced at him again, annoyed at the silence. Was he going to make me beg for his attention now?

"Taking one last look around?" I said again, as cheerily as possible.

"What's wrong?" he asked, "you look so sad".

"Oh nothing" I said, "just the wind in my eyes I think!", I chuckled. Still looking down I averted his gaze. Suddenly I felt his hand on my arm. My heart jumped.

"I'm ok, really!" I said," I'd better go, drive safe !".
As I took a step forward, I felt his hand wrap around mine. In one swift motion he pulled me into the little alley beside us.

He stood in front of me and cupped my face with his hands. My heart thumped. I looked into his eyes; my back pressed against the brick wall. With his thumb, he wiped away my tears. My gaze drifted to his lips. He leaned his face in close to mine and I felt his warmth. I took in his scent and let my eyes close for a moment. I felt dizzy. Suddenly his lips touched mine. His wet perfect lips. I wanted more. I parted my lips and felt his tongue against mine. The kiss deepened . My head was spinning. His hands glided inside my coat and over my hips, his every touch making   my heart pound harder and harder. I reached my hand around to the back of his warm neck and ran my fingers up through his soft curls. His arms enveloped me as he wrapped them around me. I had surrendered, lost control.

He broke away and took a breath. He looked at me and his eyes, his expression, had changed. I had never seen him like this before. He looked surprised, excited. I could see the adrenaline running through him. It excited me.

"I'm sorry if that was too forward of me" he whispered. I could hardly speak.

"No" I whispered back, still lost in the moment, craving him and not wanting to come back down to earth, to reality. I wanted to stay here, to bury my face in his chest. I wanted him to tell me it was all ok. I wanted him to save me. I pulled him against me and kissed his lips. He parted my lips with his. His tongue caressed mine and I could taste him. I wanted to taste all of him, it felt carnal. He pulled his mouth away and kissed my neck. His breath on my skin, his soft lips, created a ripple of tingles down my spine. I closed my eyes. His hands on my hips, I wanted them to explore my body, I wanted to give myself completely to him.
He stopped, breathless. We locked eyes. The silence spoke volumes. We didn't need to speak, there was nothing left to say. We had found something in one another, something we both knew we had all along.

I looked away and gradually became aware of my surroundings. The cold, the footsteps on the street outside the alley , the traffic . Suddenly what had just happened dawned on me. I felt confused. I felt elated. I felt shame. "So…" I said and trailed off. I didn't know what I wanted to say. I wanted him to tell me what to do. My mind was blank. I realised he still had his hands on my hips and mine were still clutching his coat. I loosened my grip and in turn he brushed his hands away.

"Well," he said, and trailed off. We both looked at each other and laughed.

"So.." I said hesitating, "I guess you need to leave soon?"

"I do" he said. He paused. "I don't want to leave things with you like this". I didn't answer.

"I was thinking, if I can get all the shots I need this by this evening, I could try to come back and see you before I leave for my flight, would that be ok?" he said.

"Of course," I said nodding.

He smiled. We hesitated, neither of us wanting to leave. I turned to start walking and he followed. We exited the alley together and stood there for a moment, looking both ways. I took a deep breath. My face felt hot.

"I'll message you later?" he asked.

"Ok" I said, "talk later". We both smiled. I forced my legs to move and slowly put one foot in front of the other. They felt like jelly. I wanted to turn back but forced myself not to. As I reached the end of the street I looked back, I didn't see him, he had disappeared into the crowd , like so many years before .

The realisation of what I had just done hit me. Had anyone seen us? What was I going to tell Lorenzo? I had cheated. I had betrayed him. I couldn't wrap my head around it. Me, I had done this. I could have said no, I could have pulled away. What was I thinking? I had no excuse. Somehow, I felt I had deserved it, someone finding me beautiful, someone who wanted me, but not like this. Had I become this person? Someone that would pretend nothing had happened and just carry on as normal. I couldn't do that, but I had to if I wanted to stay with Lorenzo. Did I want to stay with Lorenzo? I did but I couldn't lie to him. My head was spinning.

I reached the house and quickly went inside, shutting the door. I went into my bedroom, our bedroom, and changed into my track suit pants and a hoodie. I checked my watch, 2.20. I turned on my phone and there was a message from Kat. I opened it and read:

See that you and Mr. Eyes are getting along better than expected. Call me!!

Oh god had she seen us? If she had, then who else could have also seen. I would call her later, I needed to think. I made a coffee and sat on the sitting room couch, intending to watch tv. I stared into space, replaying everything in my mind over and over again. The kiss, his warmth, how turned on I had been, Lorenzo, how I had let this happen. I felt tense. I was out of sync. I didn't know where to sit or how to be comfortable. Confused, I decided to run myself a bath.I eased myself into the hot water and slowly sank into it, feelings of guilt washing over me. After what I had just done, and here I was taking a nice bath so casually. How could I have done that? What did I even want from all this? I closed my eyes. Francescos face appeared in my mind's eye. How he had grabbed me and made my heart pound, how his lips felt against mine, how his loose curls felt through my fingers, silky yet rough, how I couldn't breathe with anticipation. I remembered the feel of his hands on my body. My hand moved down, stopping between my legs. Slowly I caressed myself. I remembered his eyes, his tongue on my neck. I moaned softly. His scent, his heat engulfing me. I wanted to explode. I imagined how he would feel inside of me, his mouth on my body. It pushed me over the edge and I moaned again, coming hard, a million sparks escaping from me. I kept my eyes closed and clung on to the feeling as it slowly faded, finally extinguishing, leaving
behind it my guilty conscience as its ugliness reappeared once more.
I stayed in the bath a bit longer before getting out and getting dressed. I moped around the house. Suddenly the doorbell rang. I shuffled to the door and opened it. There was Kat.

"Hi!" she said, "sorry for dropping in unannounced but you never replied to my message earlier, so I wanted to check everything was ok?"

"Hi" I said, "I really don't know if everything's ok, come in".

I felt relieved that she was there. I needed to tell someone what was going on and since she had already seen us, I didn't have to keep it a secret from her. I was scared she would judge me, scared of what she might say or that she would be disappointed in me. She came inside and I prepared her something warm to drink. Mugs in hand we sat down.
"So" she said, what the hell is going on? I saw you guys, or at least I'm almost sure it was you, down the alley near the café? Was that you?".

"It was" I said as I bowed my head. "Look, before you say anything and before you judge me, I didn't plan this to happen. We met up for coffee and he was leaving and that was it. We even said our goodbyes and then we somehow bumped into each other when I was on my way home and ..we kissed. You know I would never want to hurt Lorenzo, and you know I would never actively go out looking for someone else. I don't know how, it just happened. I didn't stop it and now I don't know what to do and I feel like the biggest fool on earth and..."

"Stop" Kat said, interrupting me. "Ok, I know you're not a bad person, in fact you're one of the nicest people I know. I know you would never go looking for something like this. Mistakes happen, it was a spur of the moment thing. The fact that you feel so badly, well, look I know you care, and I know you got carried away. I assume he's properly left now? That's it?"

"Well," I said, "yeah he's left, but he hinted at maybe coming back one last time before he leaves, to talk ..."

"To talk?" she said, surprised. "Talk about what? Do you want to see him again?"

"I don't know" I said, "yes, no.."
"Look Mims" she said, "you don't know this man. You don't know who he is, and everything he's told you could be a big fat lie. You're happy with Lorenzo, what good could possibly come from seeing him again ?"

"I know" I said, "you're right, I don't know him, but I just have an intensity with him. Look at when we met all those years ago - and I know you don't want to hear this story again because it's so cheesy- but afterwards when I would think about that meeting I always wondered, what if? What if we had spoken then? What if we had exchanged names or numbers or what if we had gotten to know each other? That's what followed me around all these years, what if. I don't want to make the same mistake again. I know it sounds stupid, I know you probably think I'm out of my mind, but I don't know if I can leave things like this and   continue wondering what if for the next 10 years"

She stayed silent. We both said nothing for a few moments. Finally, she spoke.

"Look Mims, I love you, you know I love you. I know you can get carried away and I don't want to see you hurt. I don't want to see you destroy what you have with Lorenzo for someone you don't know, that's all."

"I know" I said, "and I feel the same, but I don't know what to do here. I don't want to lie but I also don't want to hurt Lorenzo."

"If he wants to meet again tomorrow" she   said, "then it's just for coffee I assume?"

 "Yeah, I guess so" I said.
"Ok, well meet him then" she said, "say your proper goodbyes. He's flying back to Italy tomorrow evening so it's not like this is a long-drawn-out full-blown affair. You made a mistake; you'll say your goodbyes and he'll leave. After that you can really think about what you want, I mean, does he want to be with you? Do you want to be a couple?"

"I don't think so, I mean we haven't discussed anything" I said, "it was just a kiss".

"Ok so it was just a kiss" she said, "let's not get ahead of ourselves then".

"You're right" I said feeling slightly relieved, "He'll go his own way and who knows if I'll see him again, I'm blowing things way out of proportion".

"Right" she said, "you've been with Lorenzo for years and you don't stop loving someone from one day to the next.   You made a mistake, its 10 minutes of your life".

"I guess so" I said, "I do love Lorenzo, it was a silly mistake".

 "A silly mistake" she repeated as she nodded.

We sipped our drinks. She left a couple of hours later and I started to cook dinner for myself. Lorenzo would be home late, so I ate alone and watched some TV, trying to focus on anything else except this whole situation. I went to bed early and as I was drifting to sleep my phone pinged. I   picked it up, it was Francesco. His message read:
Hey, it looks like I was able to get enough shots for what I need after all. I'm coming back tonight, and I'll leave from there tomorrow afternoon. I know you're probably working but if you have some time for breakfast or lunch I'd love to talk.
I wouldn't have enough time in the morning I thought, maybe a quick coffee at lunch, it wouldn't take long. I replied: Hey lunch sounds good, around 1, the café? He replied almost immediately: Great, see you then, sleep well.
I put down the phone and thought about what we would say to each other.

Chapter 9

The next morning, I woke up and for second my mind was blank. In a flash it all came pouring back, yesterday, the kiss, today the meeting. I felt Lorenzo in the bed beside me. He had gotten back late last night and was starting a bit later today. I tiptoed out of the room and went to make my coffee. As I drank it, I thought of the day ahead and tried to push yesterday's events to the back of my mind. I showered and dressed, putting on my green calf length skirt, black tights and my blue loose knit jumper. I tied my hair up in a messy bun as it wasn't cooperating, and I couldn't leave it down. I grabbed my bag, my coat and my scarf as I put on my shoes. The scarf suddenly reminded me of yesterday's tears. I wrapped it around me and walked out, making my way to work.
I was first to arrive and as I opened up and got inside, Kat came bouncing in behind me, coffees in hand.

"Thought you might need this" she said and smiled.

"I do thanks" I said and smiled back, taking the coffee, grateful.

"So you meeting him to say goodbye today?" she said.

"Yep, meeting him for lunch at the café" I said. "Around 1".

"Ok" she said, "well I hope it'll help you get closure".

"Me too" I said and sipped my coffee.

The morning was slow. I checked my watch every 5 minutes thinking more time had passed. It hadn't. We weren't very busy although Mondays usually weren't.
Around 12.30 my phone pinged.

Probably Lorenzo I thought, as I had sent him a message earlier wishing him a good day, joking about how we hadn't seen each other in years. As I turned on the phone, I saw it was from Francesco. Oh great, I thought sarcastically, after all that he's probably cancelling. Expecting disappointment, I read the message:
Hey, I'm stuck on a work call and I'm not sure if I'll make it down on time. There's a café in my hotel lobby, would it be ok to meet there instead? If you're busy I understand, we can also meet later if it suits you better.

I knew his hotel, it was just down the street from here, not more than 10 minutes' walk. I'll just go there I thought, get it over with.
Hey, I replied, I can come there, it's ok it's not far, I'll be there at 1?
That's great he replied, I should be finished by then, see you soon.
As I waited the long 15 minutes before leaving, the minutes ticking by, I felt butterflies in my stomach. I had resigned myself to saying our goodbyes and him leaving and us never seeing each other again and I had almost convinced myself I didn't care, but he still made me anxious. I did care.

"Ok I'm off" I said to Kat, grabbing my things.

"Ok see you later" Kat said, "good luck".

I had never been inside this hotel although I had passed it so many times. It looked fancy, sometimes there was a doorman outside. I arrived at the entrance and walked up the steps, no doorman today. Walking in I looked around for the café. I found it right past the reception on the left and headed there. It was empty apart from an elderly couple. I found a table with two chairs and sat down. I ordered a coffee and pulled out my phone. 12.55. My coffee arrived and I started to sip it. My phone pinged and it was Francesco.
Hi he said, if you're in the café I'm almost done I promise, just another 5 minutes.
Ok I replied, I'm here.

Minutes passed and he still hadn't come down. What am I doing here? I thought to myself. Waiting on this guy and he's not even bothering to show up. My time is important too. Calm down I told myself, it's not his fault. I checked my phone, 1.10. I was about to message him and tell him I was leaving when he messaged first:
I'm so sorry, I'm literally stuck on this conference call, it was supposed to end 30 minutes ago, I'm not even talking, I'm just on mute.
Ok I replied, maybe I should go then, I don't have much time.
He replied: If you have to then ok, I'm so sorry, I'm in room 207, do you have 5 minutes to say goodbye in person? I can't leave in case they call on me.

His room? I thought, jeez I wasn't expecting that.
Ok I replied.
As I left the café and walked to the elevators, I almost stopped myself. Was I really going to his room? I wanted to see him though, I didn't want to leave things like this. At the elevator doors I spotted the sign showing the different levels and room numbers.

Room 207, room 207, oh there it is, 3rd floor. I stepped onto the elevator and pressed 3. The doors closed. As it began to climb, I could feel my heart in my mouth. I'm gonna be sick I thought, I've got to calm down. With a   ding! the doors opened, and I stepped out into the hallway. I looked both ways and saw the arrows and room numbers on the wall. Rooms 201-220 to the left. I turned left and padded down the carpeted hallway. It smelled of roast potato, why did all hotels smell like that? I remarked to myself. 209,208,207 – here it was. There was a do not disturb sign on the door, should I leave? No, you fool, he told you to come up, I thought. What if he's busy though? He's not, just knock.
Before I knew what I was doing my knuckles were rasping on the door. My heart pounded.
Silence. I didn't hear any movement inside. I waited … nothing. How long had it been? I thought. I knocked again, a little bit louder this time. I winced at how loudly it echoed. I heard a shuffling inside. Suddenly there was a   loud click! and the door swung open. I felt a gush of air and there he was. Oh god there he was.

"Hi" he whispered, smiling. I could hear low voices in the background.
"I'm on mute" he said, "thanks for coming up, I should be finished soon but I know you have to go".

"It's ok" I said, "I have a little time". Still standing in the hall, a cleaning lady passed behind me with her cart.

"Come inside for a second" he said.

"Ok" I said, and stepped in as he closed the door behind me.

"I just have to be quiet in case they call my name and I need to say something" he whispered.

"Ok" I whispered back.

As I walked into the room I looked around. The curtains were opened, sunlight cascading onto the blue carpet. The bed was made, cushions propped up. I smelled soap, he had just showered I guessed as I felt the humidity radiating from the open bathroom.

"Do you want a coffee?" he asked, motioning to the small table, on top of which sat a tray with a coffee machine and cups.

"Yes, ok thanks" I said, "if it's not too loud?"

"I hope not, I haven't tried it yet" he said quietly.

He took one of the cups from the tray, placed it on the coffee machine and switched it on. His laptop was on the table too, screen open. I could make out an open application and call in progress. I tried to eavesdrop on the conversation, but it was all in Italian. I could understand quite a bit usually, able to follow a conversation, but I couldn't understand anything now. I couldn't pay attention. His presence was intoxicating and as I watched him, I wanted to reach out and touch him. As the machine flickered on it started to spurt and stutter, the noise resembling a lawn mower.

Oh no! I mouthed and smiled, putting my hands over my ears. He laughed as he tried to stop the machine from making any further noise but it just kept going. When the cup was full almost to the brim, the machine quietened, and Francesco breathed a sigh of relief.

"I'm not having one" he said with a big smile.

"We can share" I said smiling back.

"Sit where you like" he said, motioning to the empty chair beside the table and the end of the bed. I sat on the chair, took the cup from the machine and added sugar and milk. He sat on the end of the bed close to me. He looked at me and there it was, that electricity.

"Again, I'm sorry about this" he said, shaking his head.

"Don't worry, it happens" I said.

"So" he said, "about yesterday, I wanted to apologise if I was out of line, really…I know you have a boyfriend, and it wasn't right of me to initiate anything".

"I'm the one to blame" I said, "I let it happen after all". "Well, I apologise anyway" he said, "and it looks like I'll be coming here for work again soon. When I do, I'd love to see you again, I don't want things to be awkward between us".

"Thanks for that" I said, "I appreciate it, and yeah, I'd love to see you too if you come back one day, things won't be awkward. I had a great time with you and I'm happy we ended up meeting".

"Me too" he said, "I'm glad we cleared that up, I was afraid you wouldn't want to see me again".

"No not at all" I said, "we got carried away I guess, it happens".

He nodded and smiled, then jumped up and hit a key on his laptop.

"Si si" he said and proceeded to talk in Italian with the others on the call. I had never heard him speak Italian until now. I mean, I had heard Lorenzo and other people speak it so many times, it was nothing new. But with him, it was different. It had an almost musical tone to it, and that coupled with his deep voice, it was entrancing. It awakened something deep inside me. I could have listened to him for hours. God, even the way he spoke turned me on, I needed to get a grip.
He had wrapped up the call it seemed. I understood goodbye, ciao ciao, and he clicked the keyboard again.

" Done, finally" he said taking a breath.

"We don't have to whisper anymore" I said in a normal voice. He smiled. I looked at my watch and it was almost 1.45 already. I hadn't realised so much time had passed. "Oh, I have to go" I said, "sorry I didn't realise it was so late".

"Oh, no problem" he said, "Thanks for coming up".

"Of course," I said and stood up to walk towards the door. He passed beside me to open the door, and as he did, he turned to face me. With his hand on the door handle he paused.

"Well, I'll see you soon I hope" he said, as he looked into my eyes.

"I hope so too" I said.
He leaned in to kiss me goodbye. He pressed his cheek against my cheek, then moved to the other side. He lingered there. I could hear his breath. I could feel his beard brush against my skin and my body tingled. As he started to slide his face away, I turned my head slightly. Our lips touched. A jolt ran through me. Neither of us moved. Suddenly his scent enveloped me, and I wanted to devour him.

I kissed him, softly at first, savouring the softness of his lips. He kissed me back. I felt his hunger and he felt mine. The kiss deepened; our wet tongues intertwined. His hands fell to my waist, my hands found their way back to his soft hair. Fuck. I was so turned on, I couldn't catch my breath, I could feel myself getting wet. His hand glided from waist upwards to my neck, grazing my breast on its way. My body sang. Please do that again, I thought to myself. His other hand moved down from my waist to the top of my ass. The anticipation, I felt like I was going to explode. I wanted his hands to touch me, every part of me.

I slipped my hands under his jumper, placing my palms on his warm bare chest. I felt his body stiffen at my touch. His kiss deepened. I felt his fingers dance on the top of my waistband, hooking them underneath it. I was on fire. He broke away and kissed my neck. I closed my eyes and pressed my body against his. I wanted all of him. I slid my hands down and brushed the top of his jeans. His breathing became heavier and his reaction excited me even more. I moved my hand down further until it was over the bulge in his jeans, I wanted to feel his excitement for me, how hard he was for me. As I grazed it, he moaned softly. He quickly lifted my skirt and placed his hands on my thighs, slowly moving them upwards. My breath quickened. Over my tights he continued upwards until he arrived between my legs. He caressed me slowly. I wanted to rip his clothes off, rip mine off, I could have come right there and then. I felt hot and wet.

I moved my hands to his jean fly, unbuttoning it, one button at a time, fumbling. I couldn't concentrate while he was touching me like that. Our lips met, kissing again, our tongues massaging each other's, feeling more urgent now. His touch became firmer. Ripping his jeans open I reached my hand out again touching his hard bulge. He moaned softly and suddenly pulled my tights down roughly. He buried his hand in my underwear, finally touching my wet pussy, his finger caressed my clitoris. I moaned in surprise at how good it felt and grabbed a handful of his hair, tugging it gently. His finger slid inside me.
"You're so wet" he said, breathing quickly. In one swift motion he bent down and picked me up in his arms. My legs wrapped around his waist as he carried me to the bed, laying me down on it gently. One moment melted into another in a blur, a blurry wash of colours. He kissed me
and as he towered over me, he pulled his jeans down. His eyes were on fire.

 He pulled down his boxers, his hard cock springing out. Oh god his beautiful penis, I wanted to take him in mouth, to taste him. Before I could move, he bent down and pulled at my underwear firmly, sliding it and my tights down my legs before letting them drop to the floor.

My heart raced. I lifted my legs and placed my feet flat on the bed. He knelt down and pulled my legs apart softly, exposing me. I felt his breath on my inner thigh as he kissed me there, his wet tongue and lips inching their way upwards. My body trembled. I ached for him. Suddenly I felt his mouth on my pussy, his lips kissing my clitoris. I arched my back in response. I looked down at him between my legs and as we locked eyes it was enough to push me over the edge. His tongue caressing me, I was coming. My head rolled back   and I moaned as I let go, coming hard, like never before. Pleasure washing over me, as if fireworks were escaping my body.

He pulled himself away and climbed over me. As we faced each other I ran my hand up to the back of his head, running my fingers through his hair. I wanted to kiss him, to taste myself in his mouth. I reached down and wrapped my fingers around his hard cock. He moaned as I guided him towards my pussy. I felt his warm tip against me. He slowly entered me, his tip at first, and with a slow thrust I felt more of him inside me. I wanted all of him, and with another slow thrust he was fully inside of me. We both moaned as he lingered. He cupped my breast with his hand and ran his thumb over my hard nipple as he thrust again. I felt I could come again and again. His thrusts became deeper and faster. Suddenly he stilled and moaned, burying his head in my chest. Neither of us moved, breathless. We stayed there holding each other, as our passion hung in the air like a cloud above us.

I didn't know how much time had passed. Slowly, reluctantly, I was coming back down to earth. Francesco laid beside me. We still didn't speak. He took my hand and placed it in his. Work, I thought, oh god what time was it? I didn't fucking care, I didn't want to move. Once I moved it was over, I wanted to stay in this bubble. We stayed a while longer, staring at the ceiling. Finally, Francesco spoke, his deep voice gravelly.

"So maybe you can forget my apology from before, and I could make a new one?" he said. I could hear from his voice he was smiling.

"No need for apologies" I said, smiling too.
He sat up and looked at me, leaned in and kissed me. I felt a rush, I felt lightheaded. I suddenly wanted him again. I kissed him back, our tongues intertwining as our kiss deepened. I pressed myself against him. He wrapped his arm around me firmly. I felt breathless, hot. I wanted to let myself go again.

He traced his hand down my chest and over my breast, his touch making my nipple hard. He broke away from our kiss and lowered his head. He opened his mouth and slowly ran his tongue over my breast, teasing my nipple. A moan escaped me. His hand continued down my body and arrived between my legs, his fingers over my clitoris, rubbing gently. I could feel myself building already, my body moving and arching with his fingers. He slid a finger inside me, and I took a sharp breath in. It felt so good, oh god it felt good. His finger slowly slid in and out of me while his hand grazed my clitoris each time. With his tongue still teasing my nipple, I moaned, louder this time. He moved his lips to mine and pushed his tongue into my mouth. I was close. "You're so beautiful" he said in a deep voice. He sounded aroused. I opened my eyes and met his gaze. Suddenly I came hard. Moaning and tilting my head back, I shut my eyes. I could feel him watching me, it made me come even harder. I felt my skin prickle as I savoured the pleasure and willed it not to end.

I felt him remove his hand from between my legs and the bed shift. Still with my eyes closed, I felt him push himself inside of me. He thrust hard and moaned sharply. My breath quickened. He moved in and out of me firmly, faster and faster until suddenly he cried out, ah! He stilled for a moment breathless. He shifted his body and laid back down beside me on the bed. Fuck I thought, fuck fuck. This was insane, I was insane. I wanted to stay beside him, to shut my eyes and never wake up. I wished I was someone else, someone carefree with no responsibilities. I finally I looked at my watch. 2.45.
Crap, I was late, really late. I sat up.
"I have to go" I said, reaching down to collect my shoes. I stood up and pulled my underwear and tights on.

"I have to go too" he said, "I was hoping it wasn't that late".

"I wish we had more time" I said, slipping on my shoes.

"Me too" he said, "I know I'm leaving but I'll be coming back soon, for sure".

"Ok" I said, "I hope you do".

I stood back up and grabbed my coat, putting it on quickly. "Let's talk soon" I said.

"I'll message you" he said.

"Ok" I said, "I hope you have a good trip back home".

"Thanks" he said. He stood up and cupped my face with his hands. He kissed me. I hated that I had to leave, that he had to leave. I knew once I walked out that door, I would have to face another reality. I knew I was a coward; I just didn't want to face it. We held on to our kiss for a few moments, then separated and looked into each other's eyes.

"I'm so so glad I met you, again" he said. He smiled, his warm inviting smile.

"Me too" I said and smiled back. "I'll talk to you soon".

"You will" he said.

With that I walked to the door, opened it and stepped out. I looked back as I shut the door behind me and saw him standing in the middle of the room, watching me walk away. "Bye" I whispered; I don't know if he heard me. The door shut with a hard clank. I made my way to elevator and down to the lobby and walked out of the hotel into the cold air. I took my phone out of my pocket and turned it on.

5 missed calls and 2 messages from Kat. Fuck- Kat. I knew I was late; she must have been worried about me. I called her straight away. The phone rang only once and she answered.

"Mim ?!" she said anxiously, "Are you ok??". I told her I was on

my way.

One kiss was one mistake, and I could have maybe kept quiet, but this was too big. I wasn't that person; I couldn't be around Lorenzo pretending I cared for him when I had done this behind his back. I couldn't keep this secret from him. I knew it from the moment I stepped out of that hotel room. I just couldn't. I didn't know how I would tell him; I couldn't even begin to think about that. It would hurt him; I didn't want to hurt him. I wished there was another way. When would there ever be a good time to hurt him? It had to be face to face, I owed him that. I arrived at the shop and walked inside.

"There you are!"   Kat said.

"I know" I said, "sorry again, I lost track of time".
As I took off my coat and sat at my desk she said, "What's wrong Mim? you look like you've seen a ghost!"

"Oh nothing" I said, "just tired I guess". I tried not to make eye contact with her. I felt as if the word guilty was written across my forehead and couldn't bring myself to look at her.

"You seem weird" she said, "did something happen?"

"No!" I said, lying outright. I couldn't tell her, not now, I was too ashamed.
A customer walked in and to my relief it stopped any further questions. Kat spoke with her, and I continued my drawing from this morning. When the customer left, I pretended to be concentrating so that she wouldn't interrupt me and she didn't. The time ticked slowly towards 6. I was eager to get out and to get home but at the same time I was dreading it. Our home would no longer be one of love, but a broken one. At 6 I stood up and grabbed my stuff while Kat was still finishing up with something.

"I'm gonna go" I said, "I think I ate something off, I don't feel well".

" Aw ok" she said, "I'll lock up, I hope you feel better though".

"Thanks, I'm sure I'll be ok once I have a rest" I said, "have a good evening, I'll talk to you tomorrow".

"Ok talk tomorrow" she said and waved goodbye. I smiled and waved as I stepped outside. I walked briskly, like I was in a hurry. I wasn't sure why, maybe the faster I walked the less I could properly think about what had happened. I wanted to push it out of my mind.
I reached the house, and it was dark inside. Lorenzo wouldn't get home until late tonight. I twisted the key in the lock and pushed myself in, shutting the door behind me. I stood there in the dark with my back pressed against the door and took a deep breath. I closed my eyes. Our home, I thought.

I turned on the lights, removed my coat and scarf and went into our room to get changed into my sweatpants and hoodie. I put on my big woolly socks. I went into the kitchen to make myself some dinner. I was trying to follow my regular routine. I should leave Lorenzo some dinner, I thought. That made me sad. Would this be the last time I left him dinner? We often did little things like that for each other. I would leave him plates of food in case he was hungry when he got back late and didn't want to cook or leave little notes for him to find before going to work if we had missed each other the night before. If I saw something when out shopping that reminded me of him, I'd get it for him. He did the same for me. He would often send me messages during the day just to say he loved me. He was the last person on earth that deserved this.

Noticing his special cooking spoons in the jar on the counter, I felt as if I was intruding, as if I was a virus in his space and didn't belong there. I made a quick omelette and ate in front of the tv, hoping it would distract me. It didn't. I would wait up for him tonight, I thought. I laid on the couch and thought about Francesco, about our afternoon. I blushed. He was passionate, it had been passionate. I hadn't felt that way ever for someone. It was the most intense sex I'd ever had. I replayed it in mind and felt my heart pound at the memory. I could still smell him on my flesh and each time I caught his scent it sent a jolt through me. I had never been so conflicted, loving two people at the same time. I had had the most transcendent experience of my life, and it was tarred with guilt and regret.

I fell asleep in front of the tv, my body shutting down. When I woke up, I noticed faint daylight in the room. I must have slept all night. The tv was off and I had been covered with a blanket.

Lorenzo must have done that when he got home. I checked my watch, 6.30. He would still be asleep in bed. I would have to leave for work without having a chance to speak to him.

I got up and made my coffee, sat on the couch and savoured the peace. The thought of going into work, facing Kat, not having spoken to Lorenzo, and pretending to have a normal day. It filled me with dread. I felt physically sick. I couldn't bring myself to go get ready. I couldn't face it today. I messaged Kat and told her I wouldn't be coming in as I still felt unwell. She told me to take it easy and that she would be ok on her own. I felt bad, but I knew she would understand.

As I waited for Lorenzo to wake up, my phone pinged. It was Francesco:

Hi Miriam, I just wanted to let you know I've arrived back to Italy. I don't know how you're feeling about everything, but I can't stop thinking about you. I hope to hear from you. Kiss. Francesco

My heart soared instantly. I couldn't help it. Seeing him say those words, that he felt something for me, it was reassuring. I wanted to see him, to hold him, to talk with him face to face. I replied: Hi Francesco, I'm glad you arrived safe, and I feel the same. I wish you were here. Kiss I put the phone down. Lorenzo was sleeping the next room; this felt all wrong.

Around noon I heard him stirring. He's waking up, I thought, and suddenly felt anxious. He shuffled around the room for a few minutes before coming into the kitchen. I was on the couch which was right in front of our open plan kitchen, so I was able to see and talk to him as he made his coffee.

"Hi" he said sleepily.

"Hi" I said, trying to sound serious, "did you sleep well?"

"I slept all right" he said as he grabbed his cup of fresh coffee. He sipped it. "Did you? You fell asleep on the couch, so I didn't want to wake you".

"Thanks" I said, "I must have dozed off, I was quite tired". He nodded and took another sip. I had to say it, I thought, I had to do it now.

"So" I started, there's something I need to talk to you about..."

"Ok?" he said, looking up.

"I'm so sorry" I said, and as the words fell out of my mouth, tears came to my eyes.

"You're sorry?" he asked, "hey what's wrong? Did something happen?"
He put down his cup and came to sit beside me, big drops now falling from my cheeks.

"Hey hey" he said, "what's going on?", and he cupped my face with his hands. I didn't want him to be affectionate, I didn't want to make a fool of him. I took his hands and pulled them away from my face.

"I'm so sorry" I said, bowing my head, sniffling. "I've done something". Giant tears were now forming and falling from eyes.

"You did something?" he asked confused, "What do you mean? What did you do?"

"I …I… was intimate with someone else" I said. I buried my face in my hands and sobbed. I didn't want to see his reaction.
He paused. "What? he said.
"I'm so sorry" I said quietly, "it just happened".

"When??" he asked, "When did this happen?? With who? What do you mean intimate?!" he cried.

"It's no one, you don't know him", I said.

"That fucking guy, it's that fucking guy from the dinner the other night, isn't it??" he said. I could hear the panic in his voice.

"Yes, him" I said.

"Where is he?!" he said standing up. "Where the fuck is he?!"

"He's gone" I cried, "he's not here anymore, he left".

"When? When did this happen? You kissed him?" he said.

"It happened yesterday, yes we kissed" I said. He started pacing up and down the room.

"What else did you do? Did you just kiss or was there more?" he said. Hurt flashed across his face. I couldn't bring myself to say it out loud, I looked down.

"Is that all you did, Miriam?!" he asked again raising his voice.

"No" I said, so quietly it was barely a whisper.

"What ?!" he cried, "What did you say?!"

"No" I said, slightly louder.

"What the fuck?! What do you mean no? You fucked him? Is that what you're telling me ?!" he was shouting now.

"We were ... intimate, yes" I said.

"What the fuck does that mean?" he said, "Did you fuck him or not?" I put my head in my hands. My face was wet from my tears.

"Answer me Miriam!" he shouted.

"Yes" I said.

"Yes?" he shouted, "Yes??"

"Yes" I said again.

"I don't fucking believe this!" he shouted, "How? Did you do it here? In our bed??"

"No!" I shouted back, "No, he never came here!" He paced up and down.

"Where then? Where did you do it? How?!" he cried. His face was flushed, he was angry, he was hurt, I could see the betrayal he felt.

"It doesn't matter!" I cried, "I'm sorry! I'm sorry I didn't want to hurt you!"

"You didn't want to fucking hurt me??" he shouted, "Who the fuck are you right now?! Fuck you, fuck this!" he cried as he stormed off to our bedroom. I could hear him rummaging around.

This was a nightmare, and it was all my fault. Fat tears still falling from my face, I wanted to hug him, for it to all be ok again. He came out of the bedroom holding a bag and as he walked back into the kitchen, he reached down to the counter and grabbed his keys.

"What are you doing?" I said. He didn't respond as he walked to the sitting room table and snatched his phone.

"What are you doing ?!" I cried. He walked away and I heard him open the front door.

"Don't leave!" I cried. I heard the door slam and I raced to the end of the hall to see his shadow moving out of focus, down the stairs and out of sight. I stood there and bawled my eyes out. He was really gone. Could I blame him? I knew it was going to be hard but seeing him looking at me like he didn't recognise me anymore had shaken me. I had never seen him like that, and his expression haunted me. He had looked right through me. I crumpled to the floor and cried and cried until eventually, I calmed.

The rest of the day was a blur. I cried, I slept. I sent him a message after message asking him where he was, telling him that I was so sorry, and to please talk to me. He didn't respond. It suddenly dawned on me that my life had changed for good and there was no going back. The heaviness of that scared me. We had been together for so long that we relied on each other, we were partners, and now in a flash that had vanished. What would happen now? Would he move out? Would I? Could I even afford to stay by myself? Would he come back? Could we work it out? Did I want it to work out? I didn't know and I couldn't think that far ahead. I wanted him to be ok, that's all I wanted.

Chapter 10

I was still in a blur when I awoke the next morning. I felt like I was on another planet, and everything felt surreal. I remembered work. The shop felt like something I had done a long time ago, like a hazy memory. I couldn't face going outside. I had to talk to Kat. I messaged her and said I didn't think I could come in, that there was something happening with me and that I needed to see her. She responded straight away and said she would come asap. In a haze I showered and put on fresh clothes. I couldn't bring myself to look in the mirror.

Kat arrived and when I opened the door, she took one look at me and said, "Ok you need to tell me what's going on, have you been crying?". My eyes must have been red and puffy, my whole face probably too.

I let her in and tried to stop the tears. She held me and told me that it would be alright, that I could tell her anything. I told her everything. The sex with Francesco, the fight with Lorenzo, how he had stormed out and I hadn't heard from him. She listened quietly. When I was done, she hugged me tightly. She squeezed me, and I appreciated that so much. When she let go, she said "Oh Miriam, I'm so sorry".

We talked for hours; she said the shop could take a break today. She made us lunch and forced me to eat. I felt better afterwards. She told me that she understood that she was here for me whatever happened. I had been so scared to tell her, that she would be disappointed in me, it was comforting to know she wasn't.
She asked if I wanted to work things out with Lorenzo and I said I wasn't sure. I had feelings for Francesco, I was confused. She nodded and told me I would need to figure out what I wanted. I agreed. I hoped that time would tell me what I needed to do. She stayed with me until it got dark out and made me dinner before heading home. She told me to take as much time as I needed, that she would hold the fort at the shop. I thanked her and when she left, I felt a little better.

The week that followed, I had ups and downs. Lorenzo eventually messaged me and told me he was staying with a friend, and that he would be by to pick up his stuff at the end of the week. He said he wasn't ready to talk yet, and I respected that. I told him to come by whenever he wanted and that I was here when he was ready to talk. I went back to work a couple of days after that awful day. Kat was the main reason for that, as she visited me every day at lunch, and managed to lift my spirits enough for me to find the willingness to get back to a normal life. I was glad to be back.

Francesco had messaged me during that week too, asking how I was. I hadn't told him about my breakdown with Lorenzo, but we messaged each other daily. I loved talking to him, he made me feel safe and he made me laugh. It was strange being in an empty house. Even though Lorenzos hours meant we used to hardly see other, it was different after he left. I felt the emptiness, a void. I kept asking myself if I had done the right thing, not the cheating, but the ending of my relationship with Lorenzo and the ongoing contact with Francesco. Had it all been worth it?

Lorenzo came to collect his things one evening as I was getting back from the shop. He didn't look as angry as the last time I had seen him. He came inside and picked up his suitcases in the bedroom. He then proceeded to fill them with every item he owned. As he was packing, I stayed in the sitting room, not wanting to push him or pressure him into talking.

When he walked through the sitting room 15 minutes later, grabbing things as went, I asked him how he was. "Fine" he said, not making eye contact with me. I asked him if he was still staying at his friend's house and he said he was, and that he was looking for an apartment of his own. He spoke matter of factly. I asked him if we could sit down and talk, and he asked me if I was still in contact with Francesco. He looked at me for the first time as he waited for me to answer. I paused and before I could say anything he looked away and shook his head.

He continued stuffing things into his bag and then disappeared to the bedroom again. A few minutes later I heard the door slam. I walked to the hall and the bedroom was empty, he had left. I couldn't say I was shocked, I just wished he was ok.

I was still talking to Francesco every day and after Lorenzo left officially, I decided to tell him what had happened, but I didn't want him to think I was expecting anything from him. I had messaged him and said that Lorenzo knew what had happened between us, and that he had left a few days ago. He replied and said he was sorry, and he hoped it hadn't been too hard on either of us. He asked why I didn't mention it sooner. I told him I hadn't wanted to talk about it, and he respected that. He told me he missed me, and I told him I missed him too. I couldn't wait to see him again. He was working in Milan at the moment, after a few days break at his home in Palermo.

I had seen some of his work online, his photography was stunning. The way he worked with light and shadow, the colours were striking, and some photos looked like paintings. Portraits and landscapes, they were all breathtaking and there wasn't one I didn't like. He was really talented; it was no wonder he was able to freelance successfully and seemed to be in demand.

A couple of weeks passed and I still had no news from Lorenzo. Work was going well, we were busy, and Kat made me laugh so much that I began to feel better about things. I found my groove at home, my new routine. One day Francesco asked for my address, he wanted to send me something he said, just something small that made him think of me. I gave it to him and wondered what it could be, excited. We had started talking on the phone most evenings, sometimes for hours at a time. I waited anxiously and 5 days later I came home to a package in my letter box. Well, more of a packet, a large envelope. The address had been handwritten and there were a number of stamps on the back that I didn't recognise.

The package felt light but rigid. In the house I ripped it open. Inside was a white sheet of paper but it felt heavier than a regular sheet of paper. As I flipped it around there it was, a photo. A street scene, a cobble stoned windy street, with people walking up and down the footpath, some blurred and out of focus. It was in black and white but with pops of colour from people's clothes and shop fronts lining the sides of the footpaths. It was beautiful. I looked inside the envelope and found another smaller piece of paper. I took it out and it was a handwritten note. It read: A scene from one of Dublin's many city streets, taken on July 17th, 2009, right before you walked down it. I thought you'd like to have it all these years later, like I've had it with me since then.

Oh, wow I thought, I couldn't believe it, I couldn't believe him. This was so thoughtful, I loved it. I felt a warm rush. I was speechless. I messaged him straight away to thank him and to tell him I loved it. He replied and said he was glad that I did and that now we both had the same picture to remind us of each other, that is, if I didn't forget about it in a drawer somewhere! I placed it in my bedroom on top of my chest of drawers, I could get it framed I thought.

I took a picture of it and showed Kat the next day at work. When I told her what it was, of the day we had met, she rolled her eyes and laughed. "That is so cheesy, oh my god" she said. She joked around with me all the time about how cheesy I could be. I agreed though, I knew I could be, but who doesn't like a bit of cheese every now and then? One particularly stressful day at the shop, and by stressful, I mean busy with a lot of customers, and by that, I mean some very obnoxious ones, I was dying to get home. I was dreaming of putting on my comfy hoody and sweatpants, relaxing on the couch and having my evening call with Francesco. I was getting used to having the space to myself at home, I was rediscovering how much I had missed it.

It was getting close to closing time and Kat was as fed up as me. It was only a Wednesday, so we still had the rest of the week to go, but still we were glad our little shop was doing well. At 5.50 we decided to close the doors and started putting away our supplies, gathering our things to take home. "Have a great evening" she said, as I locked up. She was heading out on a date tonight. She had matched with him on her dating app and had shown me his profile earlier. He seemed like a nice guy, he was handsome. "Have fun on your date" I said, "text me when you get there and when you get back ok?". "Ok" she said, "don't worry", and smiled as she skipped off. I hadn't seen her this excited for a date in ages, maybe it was a sign. I hoped she would hit it off with someone, although she was happy as she was, it was nice to see her buzzing like this.

I locked up and made my way down the street, it was still cold, I wrapped my scarf around my neck tightly. Suddenly I felt something touch my shoulder. Without thinking I spun around. It took me a second to process what I was seeing.

There he was, Francesco.

I stared at him wide eyed for a second, he had a big smile on his face.

"Hi!" he said.

"Oh my god what are you doing here ?!" I said, hugging him. He squeezed me hard, and it felt like I had come home. I was ecstatic, I felt elated. What was he doing here? I didn't care, he was here, that was the main thing. I had missed him. After everything that had happened the last few weeks, it felt strange to see him again in the flesh. He looked exactly as he had before, but so much had changed. We separated from our hug.

"I have some work in Dublin, and since I had a few days free I thought I would come see you, I hope that's ok?" he said.

 "That's more than ok" I said, "when did you get here?" I asked.

"A couple of hours ago" he said, "I wanted to catch you before you closed the shop, so I guess I was just on time!
Are you hungry? Can I treat you to dinner?"
"I would love that" I said, and we started walking slowly together down the street. If I had known he was coming I would have at least done something with my hair I thought, or worn something a bit nicer. Oh god how did my face look? It was the end of the day so it must have looked a mess.

"What kind of food are you in the mood for?" I asked.

"Oh anything" he said. I suggested a nice quiet place around the corner that did a bit of everything. As we walked there, he told me about the work he had to do in Dublin. He would go back there in a couple of days and then go back to Italy a couple of days after that. His surprise visit had certainly cheered me up.

We found the restaurant and ordered our meal. It was nice to be able to talk to him face to face again. Everything had ended so abruptly with him, with everything, and now I felt I could take my time and really get to know him. We talked for what felt like hours, I didn't even want to think about work the next day. I wanted to enjoy myself. At a dimly lit table we sat opposite each other, a candle flickered between us.
As he talked, I watched the shadows dance across his face, his lips, his chest. I imagined kissing him. Scenes from the hotel room flashed across my mind. I squirmed. If we hadn't been in a public place, I would have jumped on him there and then. Maybe I've had a few too many drinks I thought. I'd only had two glasses of wine, but they had gone straight to my head.
Eventually we left and as we stood outside, I wondered if he would suggest continuing our date elsewhere. I thought about inviting him back to my place, but it felt strange. It was my place, but it had
been mine and Lorenzos for so long. To see him there, in our bedroom, I wasn't sure how I felt about that.

"So.." he said.

"So.." I said.

"Do you want to get a taxi home?" he asked, "I'll share it with you and get dropped off at my hotel".

"Ok" I said, as we walked to the curb to wait for a passing taxi. I liked that he didn't presume we were ending the night together somewhere, that sex was automatic. After a few minutes we flagged one down and got inside. We were going to drop me off first since my place was closer. As we sat there in the dark back seat, I remembered the last taxi ride we had shared, before anything had happened between us, and how I had felt the spark then. He sat close to me, our legs and arms touching. As we spoke, we turned our heads to face each other. There was a pause and for a moment we looked at each other. He leaned in towards me slowly, reaching his hand up to cup my face. His lips finally pressed against mine and I felt as if fireworks were trying to escape my body. We kissed slowly at first, rediscovering each other, tasting each other and savouring it. As our kiss deepened, I felt the car stop. We had arrived, too soon I thought.

"Here we are" said the taxi driver. I looked out the window to see my front door and in a moment of pure impulse, I turned to Francesco and said, "do you want to come in for a coffee?". He looked surprised and hesitated. Oh, shit I thought, I'd gone and ruined it, I had been too forward.

"Are you sure?" he asked.

"Of course" I said.

He smiled. "Ok sure" he said. He paid the taxi, and we got out. He followed me up the steps to my front door. It was definitely weird I thought, seeing him here, at my house, in this setting. I opened the door and flicked on the lights. He stepped in after me and looked around as I closed the door behind him. I lead him to the kitchen.

"Coffee? I asked.

"Yes please" he said, as he looked around. "Nice place"

I thanked him and started making the coffees. He sat at the kitchen counter watching me. I finished making two coffees. "Milk or sugar?" I asked, trying to sound normal, when all I wanted to do was take his clothes off. Honestly why was I even making coffees, I thought.

"Just black" he said. I motioned to the sitting room couch, and we walked over to sit down. I gave him his coffee and we both took a sip and placed our cups on the table. We sat close to each other. He placed his hand on my knee.

"Coffee's nice" he said.

"It's not the best, you don't have to be polite" I said, laughing.

"It's not bad!" he said, "Honestly!" I rested my hand on his shoulder and glided it down his arm. His jumper felt soft. He raised his hand and moved a strand of hair away from my face. Blushing, I looked down.
"You're so beautiful" he said. Blushing even harder I couldn't bring myself to look at him. I didn't take compliments very well. Usually, I thought people were being polite, or in the case of situations like this, that they were just saying that to get me into bed. I could never accept them as genuine.

"I hope you know that's true" he said quietly, as if reading my mind. I looked up at him, his eyes were soft. I leaned into him and kissed him.

His hand held the back of my head and our kiss deepened. His tongue caressing mine, I wanted to feel it all over me. I could feel myself getting wet already. Still kissing him, I lifted myself and quickly spread my legs as I climbed over him, resting to sit on top of him. My hands travelled across his chest and reached the bottom of his jumper. I wriggled them underneath it, and slowly started to pull it up. Raising his arms, I pulled the jumper over his head. His beautiful chest was staring back at me. He grabbed my jumper and pulled it off me, leaving me in just my bra. He kissed my chest, and his hand cupped my breast. God, it felt so good. With his finger he hooked the cup of my bra and quickly pulled it down, leaving me exposed. He placed his mouth over my nipple, his tongue brushing over it slowly, caressing me. I closed my eyes, his touch intoxicating, and ran my fingers through his soft curls as he moved his mouth to my other breast. His hands slid up my thighs.

What I would have given for him to touch me between my legs, I was aching for him. I moaned quietly. I wanted him now, I couldn't wait. I moved off his lap, and standing over him, I reached for his jeans and unbuttoned them.

He took over from me and pushed them down his legs and off. I did the same with mine. I slid my underwear down as he watched me. He did the same with his and I climbed back on top of him. Feeling the warmth of his naked body against mine, our lips and tongues met again. He slid his hands up my thighs and grazed my clitoris. I moaned; I couldn't help it. I could feel his hard cock against my pussy. I raised myself slightly and reached down. I placed my hand around his penis and guided it inside me. I sat down slowly until he was fully inside of me. We both moaned. He felt so good, I was in ecstasy.

We wrapped our arms around each other. Suddenly he picked me up and spun me around, laying me down on the couch. He buried his head in my neck, kissing me, licking me, as he thrust deep inside me. I moaned, louder this time, and he thrust again, deep and hard. I ran hand hands up his back and through his hair. He raised his head and kissed my mouth as his hand reached down. I felt his finger against my clitoris as he thrust again. He moved his finger round and round, massaging me. I could feel myself building more and more, higher and higher. His cock inside me, his fingers caressing me, his wet lips, his soft tongue. I couldn't breathe. I moaned; I was coming. I tilted my head back and moaned again, louder. A million sparks surged through me, escaped me. I closed my eyes. I felt him thrust again, harder. "Ah!" he cried, coming, and falling to rest over me, his head on my shoulder.

I didn't move, I couldn't move. I could hear my breath, heavy, satisfied.

"It's so nice to be with you again" he said, catching his breath.

"You too" I said, I missed you. He turned his head to face mine and kissed me.

"Do you want to go to bed?" I said, checking my watch. It was 11.30.

Sure" he said, "unless you want me to leave, I don't mind".

"No I want you to stay" I said.

"Ok" he said, "then I'll stay. He kissed me again and we both stood up, making our way to the bedroom. As I pulled back the covers he stood at the side of the bed, hesitating. I jumped in. He pulled back the covers on his side and slid inside.
"Do you mind if I turn off the light?" I asked. "No no" he said, as I reached back to my bedside lamp and switched it off. We laid on our sides, facing each other. He placed his hands on my waist, and I did the same, as we huddled closer together.
"Good night" I said. "Good night" he said, and I felt his lips against mine. I kissed him back and my heart pounded. Instantly I felt turned on again . His hands slid up and down my body, over my breasts, down my back, up my thighs. We caressed each other. He moved his head and kissed my neck . Kissing his way down as I closed my eyes, anticipating where he would kiss me next. He kissed my belly, then placed his hands on my inner thighs, pulling my legs apart.

>He kissed my inner thigh softly. I craved him, my heart was racing now. I .felt his lips in between my legs, kissing me softly at first, then using his tongue to caress me , softly, slowly, agonisingly slowly.

I moaned, this felt like heaven. He stopped and moved to my other inner thigh, kissing, licking his way down again. I arched my back, he was teasing me, I couldn't take it anymore. Kissing me slowly and edging closer and closer to my clitoris he finally reached it . I cried out, I couldn't contain myself, he felt so good. Almost writhing I moved my body, his firm grip on my legs holding me down. His control felt good, his taking charge. I liked this feeling of surrendering, not thinking. He continued, slowly. I felt myself building, I was going to come, it felt so intense. His tongue against my clit, the noise his mouth made as he kissed and licked me, his hands squeezing my thighs, I couldn't hold on any longer. I moaned loudly, as I came hard. Fuck I thought, fucking hell. I felt my blood pumping through my body. I opened my eyes as he started to climb on top of me. No, I thought, I want to taste him. I sat up and placing my hands on his chest, I pushed and turned him so that he fell on his back. I kissed his mouth, smelling and tasting myself on him. Wrapping my hand around his hard cock, I tugged it gently. I pushed myself down, and bowing my head I touched my lips to it, kissing him as he had done to me, softly and slowly, using my tongue. I moved his tip inside my mouth and closed my lips around it. He moaned and it turned me on. Pleasuring him, his cock hard for me as I sucked, hearing him moan, it made me want to touch myself. I pushed his cock further into my mouth as I glided my hand down his shaft. I loved how he felt in my mouth. I wanted to hear him cry out. I sucked and licked, moving his cock in and out of my mouth slowly. He reached his hand out to me, and with it moved a strand of my hair away from my face. Although it was dark the moonlight flooded the room, and he could see me. I liked that he was watching me. I looked up at him and he moaned again. Quickening my pace slightly, I grazed his tip with my tongue, and he cried out. "Ah! fuck". Breathing heavily, he suddenly sat up and grabbed me, pushing me down to the bed on my belly, my ass exposed. I felt him push the tip of his penis into my pussy, then further, and slowly more until he was fully inside of me. We both cried out. I could feel how wet I was. He held on to my waist as he quickly entered in and out of me until I heard him cry out once more. He stilled, falling on top of me, breathless. This man is fucking amazing I thought to myself, wanting to stay like this forever. He kissed me and moved off me, pulling the covers back up. I rested my head on his chest as we wrapped our arms around each other. I don't remember falling asleep.

I was awakened the next morning by my alarm. I sleepily turned it off and remembered Francesco in my bed, momentarily forgetting. He moved and opened one eye.

"It's 7 I whispered".

"Mmmm" he said, closing his eyes again.

"I have to get ready for work" I said, "you can stay if you want".

"No" he said, "I'll get up with you, walk you to work." He opened his eyes and looked at me, smiled and moved closer to me, wrapping his arms around me.

"I wish I could stay here all day" I said.

"Me too" he said, "can I see you tonight after work?"

"Of course," I said, relieved that we were both thinking the same thing. In most of, actually all of my relationships, I had always felt I wasn't on the same page as the other person. There was always a doubt. Did he feel the same way? What was he thinking? I was never sure. No man would have ever said I miss you or I want you, that never happened. I always had to read between the lines. Maybe they didn't want to show their feelings for fear of being rejected? It had been a breath of fresh air with Francesco. He had told me how he couldn't stop thinking about me, and how he was missing me. He had even sent me the photo. He wasn't afraid to say things. Even just now, he wanted to see me after work, no playing around, he was making it clear. We got up, and I showered and got dressed. When I finished, I came into the kitchen and he had a coffee waiting for me. I could get used to this, I thought. I drank my coffee while I waited for him to get dressed. Thinking about the night before made me blush, how turned on I had been. I remembered taking him in my mouth, how I had looked at him and how turned on he had been. I had never been very confident during sex, often wanting to try different things but feeling too embarrassed. With Francesco it felt different, I felt sexy. It was thrilling. Maybe his eagerness to spend time with me and his showing me his true feelings had reassured me subconsciously. Whatever it was I liked it and I hoped it continued. I hadn't felt like this in, well never. Lost in thought, I was floating on air. He emerged from the bathroom, got dressed, and we headed out. As we walked to the shop, he put his arm around my shoulders. I felt a rush of pride.

"Is this ok?" he said.

"Of course," I said, "Why wouldn't it be?"

"Well, I just wasn't sure, in case I don't know, in case you didn't want to be seen with someone else, with Lorenzo around, I don't know really".

"No, not at all" I said smiling. Lorenzo, I thought, he hadn't even crossed my mind since last night. I had thought it would feel strange having another man in the house, sharing the bed, but I had been so preoccupied I hadn't noticed anything.
I wondered if Lorenzo would be upset at seeing us. I certainly didn't want to flaunt Francesco in his face. I doubted he would be around anyway, he never went into town much and he was working most of the time, it would be such a coincidence if we ran into each other. Francesco and I walked, huddled close to together. I wished we could spend the day together.
"What are you doing today?" I asked.

"I was thinking I would have a look around here" he said, "maybe see if I can take some shots".

"Oh, good idea" I said, "although I'm not sure there's much to see around here".

"There's plenty" he said smiling, "if you look hard enough".

I smiled. "Do you want to have lunch if you're not too busy?" I asked.

"That sounds great" he said, "let's message each other later, just in case I'm getting some good shots and can't leave".

"Ok sounds good" I said, as we arrived at the shop. We let each other go.

"Have a good day" I said.

"You too" he said. We hesitated. I leaned into him and kissed him. He smiled and waved as he walked away. I opened the shop as Kat hadn't arrived yet. I was secretly glad she hadn't seen the show we had just put on outside, arriving up with our arms around each other and kissing each other goodbye – she would have had a long list of questions. I went inside and turned on the lights. As I sat down, Kat came bouncing in.

"Heeeey!" she said. She was in a good mood.

"Heeeey" I said.
"Quite a show you were putting on there with Mr Eyes" she said sarcastically as she raised one of her eyebrows.

I laughed, "You saw that?" I said.

"I sure did" she said, "so are you guys an item now or what?"

"I don't know" I said, "I mean we haven't discussed it yet but yeah, we are seeing each other again later, and he came here especially to surprise me last night, so I'm almost sure we are heading in that direction".

"Ok" she said, "well I just hope this is what you want, and that nobody gets hurt".

"I hope so too" I said.

The day was slow and quiet, but that suited me. I was a bit tired after last night, and I could just sit there and pretend I was concentrating on my drawing when actually I was thinking about Francesco and last night on a loop. I couldn't wait to see him again later. Around lunch time he messaged me before I got the chance to and told me he had made his way to the next village where he was getting some good shots. While the light was still good, he was going to stay for another couple of hours. I was a bit disappointed at missing him for lunch, but I didn't mind too much, I would have all evening with him. I went for lunch with Kat, and she pressed me for all the details of the night before. Her date had gone well, and she was seeing the guy again at the weekend. I was pleased she had found someone she liked.

I didn't go into too much detail about my date with Francesco, only to say that he had spent the night and it had been fucking amazing. "Don't get too carried away!" she said. I laughed but it was true, I did tend to get carried away, but he was the real deal. I didn't see any red flags. Granted I was more attracted to him than I had been with anyone before, and the sex was out of this world, but I didn't have blinders on either. I knew that it was easy to get swept up.

At the end of the day as we were closing the shop, I messaged Francesco to see what time he wanted to meet for dinner and if he had a place in mind, or a type of food ÿ he was craving. He said he had planned to meet me at the shop when we closed up, but that he was waiting on a call from his boss. He asked me to meet me at his hotel and we could decide then where to go. I agreed and told him I would go home first to change and then head down to his hotel. He replied with his room number in case he wasn't finished yet,104, and said if he wasn't in the lobby waiting for me then to just go up to his room. His hotel room again, I thought. I got home.
and went to shower quickly, nervous and excited to see him. I got dressed and slipped on my silky pleated turquoise calf length skirt, and a loose grey v neck jumper. Feeling sexy, I decided not to wear anything underneath, just my bra. Instead of tights I wore stockings, and I chose my silky frilly underwear. I surprised myself with my choices as normally I would have been too self -conscious.

After fixing my hair, putting some light powder on my face and some mascara, I wrapped up in my big scarf and my coat and headed out the door. I decided to walk as it would calm my nerves and after about 30 minutes I arrived. The entrance and lobby reminded me of when I had been he re last, when we had slept together for the first time and my heart began to beat faster.

Chapter 11

I walked into the lobby and looked around; I didn't see him. I walked around making sure he wasn't seated in any of the couches and then made my way to elevators. I double checked his room number and made my way to the 2nd floor. I padded down the carpeted hall, noticing how warm it was here. It was always so warm in hotels I thought, trying to distract myself from my nerves. I knocked on his door and moments later it swung open. I felt my nerves dissolve as I saw his face and soft curls.

"Hi!" he said enthusiastically, seemingly happy to see me. It made me feel at ease.

"Hi" I said, "are you ready to go?"

"My boss hasn't called yet, he's late again, he's always late" he said in an irritated tone.

"That's ok" I said, "don't worry, do you have to wait?"

"I do" he said, "The call won't take long at all, he just wants to check in, no more than a few minutes, I just have to wait here."

"You can't take the call on your phone from outside?" I asked, a little confused as to why he had to stay in the room.

"I can" he said, "but I need my laptop beside me, it has all my files and shots in case I need to send them straight away".

"Ok" I said.

"Come in" he said, "hopefully he'll call soon, it should be any minute now, sorry about this".

"Don't worry" I said smiling.

As the door shut behind me, I walked inside, adjusting my eyes to the dimly lit room ahead. He walked alongside me and suddenly, he pushed me against the wall, firmly but gently, and cupped my face in his hands. He leaned in and kissed me. His kiss felt urgent. Our kiss deepened quickly as my fingers found their way back through his soft curls. He slid his hands down to my waist, grazing my breasts on his way. My body sang. I was getting wet already. I wanted him right then and there. I moaned softly as our tongues intertwined. He placed one hand under my knee and lifted it high to his waist, pressing me against the wall. It was all happening so fast, his excitement for me turning me on. I pressed my body back against his. Holding my leg, he slipped his other hand under my skirt and placed it between my legs, caressing me over my underwear. My breathing became heavier. Fuck, this felt so good, I thought. We were both so hungry for each other.

Suddenly I heard a ringing sound, coming from far away, it felt like I was under water. I ignored it, too focused on his touch, I moaned. I heard it again. He stopped and pulled away from me. "It's my boss" he said, "I have to answer". He kissed me and I tried to make it last as long as I could, before he broke away again and ran to answer his phone which was lying on the table across from the bed. "Ciao" he said, fixing his hair and clearing his throat. He sat on the chair beside the table facing the bed. He motioned for me to sit down.

Trying to compose myself I walked over to the end of the bed and sat down, adjusting my position a few times to get comfortable. Listening to him talking Italian my mind wandered to what we had just been doing, and I couldn't wait to continue. My face felt hot. I looked around the room and turned my attention to the top of the bed. Taking off my shoes, I scooted myself up to the top. I would be more comfortable this way, I thought. My legs out in front me and a pillow against my back, I sat, taking a breath. I looked at Francesco and he was quiet, as he listened to the person on the other end of the line.

He was looking at me. I could see a fire in his eyes, I could tell he was still aroused. I still felt wet. I squeezed my legs together and looked away. I looked up at him again, unable to avert to avert my gaze for long. The table lamp casting shadows that were bouncing off his loose curls, his deep voice, his presence.

I felt a surge of adrenaline coarse through me as his eyes were on me, I liked it. Without thinking, I brought my knees up towards my chest, keeping my feet flat on the bed. My skirt fell around my waist exposing my legs. I parted my knees just a little. I felt sexy. He was fixated on me now, watching. He spoke in Italian and sounded distracted. I parted my legs just a little more, he could see my silk panties now. He stared. Watching him, distracting him, excited me even more. I held his gaze as I slowly glided my hand down to my panties, caressing myself softly over them. His eyes followed my hand as he continued to stare. They were soaked through. I closed my eyes without meaning to and when I opened them, he was wide eyed. He spoke on the phone again, his eyes not leaving me, and I heard him say goodbye, "ciao". He hung up quickly. He stood up and paused. "You're so fucking beautiful" he said, as he stepped to the end of the bed. He reached forward and grabbing my hips, he pulled me to the end of the bed. He raised my knees and parted my legs firmly as he knelt down. He kissed the edge of the stocking on my inner thigh, and slowly made his way to my soaked panties. He licked me as he went, his tongue and lips edging their way. My body trembled. He kissed my wet panties, his head between my legs. I could feel his tongue through the material, I was at his mercy. I closed my eyes with anticipation. He hooked his finger inside my panties and with a downward motion he grazed my clitoris. "I like that you're so wet for me" he said with his deep voice, and with that I could feel myself about to come. This was so hot, he was so hot. I felt so charged. I moaned and saw that fire in his eyes. With one swift motion he removed my panties and placed his mouth on my wet pussy, his tongue caressing my clitoris. I was so close. His tongue, fuck, his tongue. He moaned and it excited me even more. I felt him slide his finger inside me while his other hand reached up under my jumper. Gliding over my breast, suddenly he pinched my nipple. Fuck, oh god ,fuck ah ! I thought. I came hard, it felt so intense, so dirty, so liberating, so sensual. I opened my eyes as he stood up, quickly unbuttoning his jeans, not looking away. I loved that he wanted me so badly. He pulled down his jeans and boxers and his hard cock sprang out, his beautiful cock. I wanted him in mouth again. Before I could move, he pushed my knees up to my chest firmly and entered me thrusting hard. We both cried out. God, he feels so good, I thought. Still holding me firmly he moved in and out me hard, I liked it, I liked his hunger. Moving faster and faster suddenly he cried out "fuck ah !" as he came. Panting and breathless he fell on top of me, and I closed my eyes. That was insane I thought. I never want to leave this fucking bed.

"Don't do that to me again!" he said laughing, kissing my face, my neck, my chest.

I laughed. "Ok, I won't" I said.

"No wait, no" he said, "definitely do that again". We both laughed.
We stayed in bed and relaxed. I'm not sure how much time had passed before I suggested getting something to eat, after all, it was what we had been meeting up for in the first place, before we got sidetracked. We eventually dragged ourselves downstairs to the restaurant, ate as quickly as possible it felt like, before returning to his room where we spent the night together, fucking and sleeping. He was leaving the next day. I was happy that he had wanted to see me, and that we could spend this time together. My heart sank when I thought of him leaving again. I was falling in love with this man.

The next morning, we said our goodbyes. I tried not to show him how I was really feeling, that I was devastated he was leaving. He told me he didn't want to leave, and that if he had a choice he would stay. While I understood he had work to do, I wanted to ask him to stay, but I knew I couldn't. He would try to come back as soon as he could, he told me while we held each other.

Not wanting it to end, I clung on to him, not wanting to say goodbye. We kissed and hugged and kissed again, until it was time to leave. I walked out of his hotel and made my way to work, feeling high from our time together, but at the same time feeling incredibly low from having left him and not knowing when we would see each other again. I wished he would run out after me, like they do in the movies, but he didn't. I arrived at the shop and tried to distract myself for the day, talking with Kat, drawing, talking with customers.
I tried not to, but I checked my phone often in case I got any news from Francesco. Nothing came through from him the whole day. That evening, feeling sorry for myself, I laid on the couch watching tv. Finally a message from Francesco came through. He said that he had arrived that morning, he had been taking photos all day and had just gotten back to his hotel room. He seemed quite cool, which I resented because I was so down in dumps. Maybe he doesn' t feel the same I thought.

I resented him even more, and myself for getting carried away. I told him to have a good evening, trying to sound cool too. As I went to bed that evening, Francesco messaged me again. He said he missed me, I felt relieved. I told him I missed him too and I didn't want to wait weeks to see him again. He said he wouldn't be able to wait that long either and that he would sort something out when he got back home. I hoped he would. I wanted to be back in our bubble.

Over the next couple of weeks my feelings for him were getting stronger and stronger, as I missed him more and more. I thought about just jumping on a plane and surprising him, but I didn't even know where he lived. I'd have to wait. We spoke on the phone every night as we had done before, and I looked forward to it every day. I told him I was falling for him during one of our conversations and he told me he felt the same. He was planning to take some time off from work, and then he could come back here, or I could go there to see him. I couldn't wait. He spoke about how he would show me around his hometown, show me the sights, what we would eat, the best places to watch the sunsets and the sunrises. It was all I thought about.

Finally, after three weeks he had news. He would be able to take 2 weeks off starting the next week, and he had already checked flights and I was welcome to come when I wanted. I was ecstatic. I called Kat straight away to tell her and she was excited for me. "Finally!" she said, "now you can stop moping around!". We laughed. I had been a bit down since he left so I was sure I hadn't been the best company. I hadn't felt like doing much really. Everything reminded me of Francesco, and I thought I was losing my mind. I couldn't wait to have two whole weeks with him. I knew it sounded crazy, to fall in love with someone after such little time. But it was real, what we felt for each other, our connection. Excitedly I looked at the flights, and over the next couple of days I made arrangements. I took 2 weeks of holidays off work. Kat would be alright on her own now the shop was doing well, and we were more established. I would be leaving in a few days, arriving to Italy, and then taking a smaller flight to Sicily. He would meet me there. I got myself a hotel. I knew it seemed strange to take a hotel, but I wanted to be cautious, I had never been to Sicily, I had never seen any part of his life, and so even if I never used the hotel, I just felt more comfortable having it there as a backup. I was excited about the trip, and Kat and I talked about it nonstop. She came over a couple of times to help me decide what to wear, what to pack. I needed outfits for the evening if we went out, causal outfits, warm, cool, everything just in case. I needed her help though, as usually when I packed, I brought a ton of stuff I didn't need. It happened every time.

One time I went on a trip to Spain during the Summer and knowing it would be 40 degrees and scorching hot, I decided to stuff half my suitcase with cardigans and jumpers "in case" it got chilly. It didn't.

Kat was great because she knew what I was comfortable wearing and what I looked good in.
She made me unpack most of my suitcase and thankfully I ended up with a much better selection. I was counting down the days until I left.

I hadn't heard from Lorenzo apart from a few messages here and there. He didn't want to sit down and talk, although he did admit that he had felt our relationship was faltering towards the end.
There had been no romance anymore, and he felt that too, not just me. He was hurt from how it had ended, and I understood that, it wasn't what we had deserved as an ending. I told him I was sorry for that, and it had never been my intention to hurt him. From those few broken conversations, I could tell he was still hurt, but as time passed I could see he was moving on. Neither of us mentioned working on the relationship or getting it back, and so we both just accepted it was over. I hoped that we would be able to sit down together one day, just to talk as friends. I knew he would never forgive me, and I didn't expect him to, I just wanted to us to be friends, and if not friends then amicable at least. After being with someone for so long it was strange not to know what was going on in their life anymore, not to be a part of their narrative.

The day before I left for Italy I went out with Kat for dinner. She offered to treat me to a nice night out as a sendoff. We went for dinner and then had some drinks at a nearby pub. I was buzzing. I was so high thinking I would see Francesco the next day. My flight was quite early in the morning, so I didn't want to stay out too late or drink too much. "Wet blanket", Kat called me, when I told her it was time for me to go home. Laughing, I thanked her for the dinner and the lovely night and promised I would call her the second I landed and keep her updated the whole time I was there. I got a taxi home and went to bed, alarm set and suitcase in the corner packed, just a few more items to be put inside it last minute. I fell asleep eventually, my mind racing. I was so nervous and anxious. The thought of seeing him, of being in a beautiful place and exploring it with him. How would the trip go? What if I was making a mistake? What if something happened? I tried to silence my thoughts. I always became anxious before a trip, thinking of all the worst-case scenarios, I would always freak myself out. I knew there was nothing to worry about.

It would be perfect, I thought, as I drifted to sleep.

The next morning my alarm rang, and my eyes sprang open. I hadn't been in a deep sleep. I had given myself plenty of time to have a coffee, shower and get dressed before getting the bus to the airport. My heart was beating fast with excitement as I got ready and put the last items in my suitcase, zipping it up. I checked and double checked everything before leaving the house, making my way to the bus stop.

The bus was a few minutes late – my mind racing again with thoughts of missing my flight, but it arrived a few minutes later. Looking out the window on the way to the airport distracted me, and I took a breath. Arriving at the airport, I checked my bags in and made my way to the gate. Looking around at all the people waiting at my gate with me, Italians mainly, and hearing them, made my heart flutter a little. They reminded me of Francesco, and it made everything seem that little bit more real. I was really travelling to see him, it felt crazy and right at the same time. The flight wasn't long, and I was eager to get there and catch my second flight. I hoped I would have enough time to make the connection and that my bag would make the connection too. If it didn't arrive, I wouldn't have anything, and I needed everything in there. My underwear, my clothes and hairbrush, my creams and well, everything was a necessity especially under the circumstances. The plane landed and after some fumbling around with the doors by the air hostess, it finally opened and we spilled out onto the tarmac, making our way to the customs desk.

Luckily there wasn't much of a queue and as soon as I had passed the check, I quickly made my way through to the connecting flights area and found my gate for Palermo. The final flight was only going to be about an hour long.
I messaged Francesco to tell him I was about to board, and I would be there soon, and I messaged Kat to tell her the same. We boarded fairly quickly and before I shut my phone off Francesco replied: I'll be there, can't wait to kiss you...
I smiled to myself and turned off my phone. Bliss, that's what I felt as the plane took off. I would see him in less than an hour. Just pure elation.

Chapter 12

The plane landed, and after what felt like forever, the doors opened, and I made my way inside to baggage claim. I looked anxiously through the glass windows as I waited for my bag, to see if I could spot Francesco waiting for me outside, but I could only see a blur of faces. I turned on my phone and messaged Kat that I had arrived while I waited for my bag. The airport was small and so the bags arrived quickly.

As I wheeled it towards the exit, I felt my blood rush to head, my cheeks flushed, I was so nervous. The automatic exit doors opened, and I searched the crowd for Francesco. I had always hated this part, the searching. I walked past a line of people leaning on the metal bar in front of the exit, and made my way out and around, still searching. I walked towards the airport exit, looking around almost frantically now.

Where was he? I walked outside and leaned my suitcase beside me while I took out my phone. No messages from him. I messaged him: Where are you? I'm outside. I put the phone back in my pocket. Maybe there was traffic, I thought. A few minutes passed and still nothing. I watched people walk in and out of the airport, I watched the cars too in case I saw him. I thought I saw him a couple of times, but it wasn't him. After about 10 minutes I called him. It rang and rang and he didn't pick up. Maybe he's still driving I thought. I waited another 10 minutes, trying him again, and again it rang out. I messaged again, I'm here, where are you, are you delayed? I still felt anxious about seeing him, and that feeling had taken over. I was sure he was delayed in traffic; he had always told me how bad it was here. He would be here soon I thought, and I imagined seeing him, playing that moment again and again in my mind. I wondered if I looked ok, if he would be happy when he saw me. I checked my phone again, nothing.

I waited and waited; an hour passed. I started to get worried, had something happened? Had he changed his mind? No, I thought, don't be silly, how could he have changed his mind? I had literally spoken to him an hour ago, and I was sure he was on his way. I checked his message again for any clues, or something I might have missed or misunderstood. Nothing there to say he wasn't on his way.

I wasn't sure what to do. Should I wait longer, I thought? I tried calling again and it still rang out. What if I left and he showed up? I decided to wait another half hour and then leave, I had the hotel, I could tell him I was going there. I phoned Kat and told her he hadn't shown up yet. She was surprised but stayed positive. She told me to wait a bit longer and then make my way to the hotel. She sounded a little worried but didn't want to show it. I told her I would keep her updated.

After 40 minutes, I tried calling him again and he still didn't pick up, so I made my way to the row of taxis on the opposite side of the street and got in the first one, giving the driver the address of my hotel in the city centre. I messaged Francesco, telling him it had been almost 2 hours, so I was going to the hotel. I gave him the name of it again and told him to find me there, or at least to call me to let me know if everything was ok. I sat back in the taxi, phone in hand, and looked out the window. What was going on? I thought. I hoped that everything was ok.

What could have happened? I imagined the worst, a car crash – what if he had been injured? What if nothing had happened and he had just changed his mind? Maybe he had left his phone at home by accident and then had gotten stuck in traffic with no way to contact me? We passed a blur of buildings, people going about their everyday lives. I was angry, I was worried, I didn't know what to think. I just wanted to get to the hotel and gather my thoughts. The driver stopped and I recognised the hotel from the pictures. It was a beautiful old building on a main street in the city that had been renovated. You could tell it was seeping in history, I loved that. I paid the driver and got out of the car, while he got my bag from the trunk.

"Grazie" he said, as he handed it to me. "Grazie" I said and made my way inside. Once I had my room key, I quickly found the room on the second floor and went inside, shutting the door behind me. I felt alone suddenly, empty. I looked at my phone, still nothing from Francesco. I did have a couple of messages from Kat asking what was happening. I tried calling Francesco again, and still it rang and rang. I messaged Kat to tell her I was at the hotel and would talk to her later. I sat on the bed with a million thoughts running through my head.

If something had happened to him, how would I know? How could I even find out? I didn't speak any Italian. Should I call the hospitals? Was I being dramatic? I decided to wait another hour or at least until enough time had passed, that if he had somehow forgotten his phone at home and arrived at the airport to see I had left he would make his way back home to get in touch with me. A couple of hours, I thought. What a mess. I was convinced this was the most logical thing to have happened. I imagined him calling after a couple of hours, or showing up here, explaining what had happened. We would laugh at this silly mix up, and finally start our holiday together. I imagined kissing him, holding him, being relieved he was ok, and comforted to be in his arms.
I unpacked my suitcase, keeping my phone beside me the whole time.

By 4pm, more than two hours had passed. I had tried messaging and calling him a handful more times, and still nothing. I felt angry. If he had just changed his mind or hadn't been bothered about meeting me, who was he to be treating me like this? I didn't need this, I wasn't going to wait around for him, I thought. If I didn't hear from him by tonight, I was leaving. I rattled around the hotel room, not wanting to leave in case he came by, feeling resentful for being stuck there. At around 6pm I ordered some food. If he thought he was going to casually swing by when it suited him, then he could think again, I wasn't going to wait around, I was eating now. Rage was building inside me.

How dare he? Fuck him, I thought. I'm not going to stay here and let him pick and choose when it suits him to see me. Did I really know him? What did I really know about him? I didn't have his address. He had vaguely mentioned a street name once during one of our phone conversations but there was no way I could remember it. I didn't have any other information other than his name. It reminded me of when we didn't know each other, after we had met that first time in Dublin. How I had no details about him and wondered if I'd ever see him again, he was just gone, as if he had never existed.

I ate and tried to distract myself, calling Kat, having the tv on in the background. She thought maybe something had happened, but agreed I should wait a little in case it was a misunderstanding. I felt sorry for myself, I felt silly, as if I had misread something or believed something that wasn't there. I went from being worried that something had happened to him to being furious he had left me. I was lost.

My mind went around and round in circles.

At around 11pm, with still no news, I decided he must be in danger. I looked up the nearby hospitals on my phone and jotted the names down, as well as his name, and walked down to the reception. I had no Italian but maybe they could help? I approached an older woman working behind the desk.

"Hi" I said, "I was wondering if I could ask your help?"

"Hello" she said, "Of course, how may I help you?"

"This might be a bit strange" I said, "but I was supposed to meet someone at the airport this afternoon, and that person didn't arrive, and I can't get in touch with him. I'm worried something has happened to him".

She nodded and tried to hide her surprise; I could tell she was preparing herself for a weird request.

"I was wondering if you could call these hospitals for me, and check if he has been admitted to any of them today?" I continued, showing her the slip of paper in my hand with the names of the hospitals. She scanned them and I could see the recognition on her face.

"This is his name" I said, pointing to Francesco's name. She looked at the paper for a few moments, for longer than I would have expected, I supposed she was trying to figure out what to say. She took the paper from my hand slowly, still fixated on it.

"Okay" she said, "We are a bit busy now, but I'll see what I can do a bit later. What's your room number?" I told her and she said she would call me once she had news. I thanked her and as I walked back to my room I wondered if she would actually call.

At least I would know then for sure. Fuck I thought, what the fuck is going on? Once I got back to my room I put on my pyjamas and got into bed, turned off the tv and tried messaging Francesco again. Is everything ok? I wrote, please let me know, I'm worried.

I must have dozed off from the stress of it all because at midnight the hotel phone rang loudly. I sat bolt upright and realised where I was. I grabbed the phone, "Hello?" I said.

"Hello, this is Laura from reception" the girl said, "I'm just calling you about your request from earlier?"

"Oh yes" I said, "thanks for calling me, were you able to call any of the hospitals?"

"Yes" she said, "I called every hospital on your list and two local smaller clinics here that you may have missed, and nobody by this name is there or has been there today".

"Oh", I let out a sigh of relief, "oh that's good news, thanks so much for calling for me, really you've been a big help."

"It's no problem" she said, "have a good night Miss".

"Thanks, you too" I said, and hung up the phone.

I didn't know what to make of that information. He wasn't in hospital, that was good news, but then where was he? What do I do now? I didn't know anybody I could call; I didn't know anybody that he knew that could check. My mind spinning, I laid back down and closed my eyes. I would have to decide in the morning, maybe I would hear from him during the night.

I dozed off again and woke up the next morning at 7am. I checked my phone in the darkness of the room, still nothing. If I wasn't going to see him, I didn't want to be here. I wasn't going to enjoy sightseeing and pretending everything was normal for two weeks on my own, that wasn't happening. I wanted to go home. Why make me come all the way here to just ghost me the second I arrived?

Nothing made sense, this whole situation didn't make sense. I got up and paced around the room. I showered and dressed. My heart sank at seeing the clothes I'd brought. I felt embarrassed, remembering how excited I had been to come here. I sat on the bed and started looking at flights. If I did want to leave, then were there even flights available. I scoured the timetables and saw there was a flight leaving that evening, connecting through Italy and back home. The next one after that would be in 2 days' time.

That meant that either I left today, or I left in 3 days. What would I do here for 3 days on my own? I just wanted to get out of here. I tried calling Francesco again, still no answer. I checked the messages I had sent him, still unread. I called Kat and updated her on what was happening, which was nothing new really except that he hadn't had an accident. She didn't know what to say but said that if I didn't want to stay there alone, then to just come back and I could continue to try to get in touch with him when I was home. I booked the flight for that evening.

Once it was booked, I felt confused, disappointed. Not knowing what was going on, I couldn't really process it. I didn't know who to blame, if this had been intentional or not. I wondered if I was doing the right thing but the thought of being here in this hotel room alone for another 3 days filled me with dread.

I packed my bag and got something to eat downstairs in the café. I passed by reception and told them I would be leaving today instead of in 2 weeks' time. They were surprised but didn't press me for any details which I appreciated. I didn't want to talk to anyone. I went back to my room to wait. I felt gutted. All that buildup, for nothing. I felt like a stupid fool.

Fighting back the tears, it was time to go. I got my stuff together and left the room. I checked out at reception and went to wait outside while they called me a taxi. It arrived almost immediately, and I climbed in as the driver put my suitcase in the trunk. It was the same driver I had had the day before. I prayed he wouldn't recognise me. As we drove off, he looked in the rearview mirror. "Short trip, eh?" he said, smiling. Fuck, I thought. "Yeah" I said, forcing a smile as I chuckled weakly. Looking out the window, I prayed he wouldn't ask me any more questions. We rode to the airport in silence. The closer we got the more I fought back tears.

As we pulled up outside the airport, seeing it again, remembering myself there just hours before waiting for Francesco, my heart sank. I paid the driver and went inside to check in, and then made my way to the gate to wait for my first flight home. I couldn't believe this was happening. I was in shock. I tried not to look at or make eye contact with anyone. I just wanted to be home, to make sense of all this. I boarded the plane and sat in my seat, buckling my belt. I took my phone out so that I could switch it off. I turned the screen on and saw Francescos name flash on the screen. Reeling, I saw a message had come through from him. What the hell? I thought, as I scrambled to unlock the screen. I opened the message and stared in disbelief.

I'm sorry, it said.

Chapter 13

I'm sorry? I thought. What the fuck? I texted back straight away: Sorry? What's going on? Where are you? I hit send and waited, my eyes fixed on the screen. I felt numb.

Rejected. I waited, willing him to reply. Suddenly I heard a woman's voice – "Excuse me but you'll have to switch your phone off now as were getting ready for take-off" she said. I looked up, dazed – "Oh ok" I mumbled, and stared at the screen again before reluctantly switching it off.
I kept it in my hand and as the plane took off, I frantically tried to connect the dots. What did this all mean? Did he not want to be with me anymore? Why tell me this way? Why make me come? Why leave me in limbo and just say sorry, offering no explanation? How could he do this to me?

I spent the rest of the flight, my next flight and until I got home in a state of bewilderment. I turned my phone on again after both flights had landed and hadn't heard from him. When I finally got home and closed the door behind me. It all hit me at once. Being back home, where I had just been the day before planning my romantic getaway, and seeing everything as I had left it, I felt dejected. I felt like a fool. I had given myself completely to this person, I had bared myself, I had been vulnerable because I believed in our spark, and all for what? I felt so stupid. Typical me, I thought, always wanting to believe in something so much and then being heartbroken when it all fell apart. I wished I was someone else. When we had met each other again it was as if destiny had existed after all. I should have seen it for what it was, a chance meeting, a pure coincidence. Typical guy sees the opportunity and takes advantage, a quick fuck when he was in town, meanwhile I was thinking he was my soulmate. I had to get a grip I thought, people were shitty, and they would always be shitty.

I couldn't face talking to Kat yet. I knew she would be thinking I told you so, even though she would never tell me that to my face. I couldn't face unpacking my stupid clothes from my stupid fucking suitcase. The stupid clothes that I had thought were so fucking important, getting dressed up for him. Fuck, you fucking fool Miriam.

The anger rising inside me, I threw my suitcase on the ground and unzipped it roughly. Grabbing handfuls of clothes I threw them in the hamper, shoving them in, pushing them down. The tears finally coming, sobbing now, I grabbed handfuls of the bottles of creams and shampoos and flung them into the sink with force. "Fucking fool!" I said out loud, grabbing anything I could from the suitcase, flinging it as hard as I could against the walls. As I stood up over my now empty case, something caught my eye. The photo on my dresser, proudly displayed, a reminder of my naivety and my gullibility. Before I could think, I launched myself towards it, yanking it off the top. "You fucking fool!!" I screamed, as I tore the picture in half. I sobbed harder seeing the photo like that, ripped, I could hardly catch my breath. I tore it again. Fuck this picture, I thought, as I continued shredding it. Its pieces fell around me like confetti. When the last piece fell to the ground I grabbed the case and threw it into the wardrobe, slamming its door as hard as I could. I walked out into the kitchen and buried my face in my hands. I sobbed and sobbed. I felt as if the world was crumbling around me, beneath me. I wanted it to be over, I didn't want to think anymore. I wanted to close my eyes and sleep and wake up and realise it had all been a bad dream.

My phone pinged and for a split second I hoped it was him. I fumbled in the pockets of my coat that was strewn over the couch and found it. I switched the screen on and saw a message from Kat asking if I had gotten home ok. "Fuck!!" I shouted and threw the phone against the wall. I wasn't thinking straight, I was in such a rage, even more so now that for that split second I had hoped it was him, I was fucking pathetic. I needed to calm down.

I went to the bathroom and took a hot shower, my eyes puffy from crying. The heat felt nice against my skin, and I felt a little bit more normal. I stayed under the water until the hot water ran out. Then I got out and put on some clean pyjamas and wrapped up with extra jumpers and a big scarf. I just wanted cocoon. I laid on the couch and turned on the TV, wanting to be numbed. I sporadically burst into tears as feelings of hurt washed over me. Waves of memories, little snippets of conversations, fragments of our time together entered my mind unwanted. I felt so betrayed. Ironic really, as I had just betrayed Lorenzo, maybe this was karma. An eye for an eye.

I was sick of crying, sick of always being on the cusp of something great and having it ripped away from me. I could never just have it, there was always a catch. Or I could have it but just a taste. I was sick of it. Why couldn't things just work out. They seemed to for everybody else. I went back to work after a couple of days and before I did, I told Kat everything and she consoled me as she usually did. She couldn't work out what it had all meant either.

I kept to myself in the weeks that followed, being jovial and good humoured around Kat and at the shop but crumbling at home. I needed time. I hadn't heard from him since that day.

As more time passed, I slowly came out of my fog and accepted that I had been betrayed. I became angry with him, vowing that if I ever saw him or heard from him again I wouldn't speak to him. I didn't want anything to do with him. I slowly built my walls back up.

After a few months had passed, I had resigned myself to never seeing him again. I reduced our whole whirlwind relationship to a live and learn lesson – a lesson to not be so trusting of people. Still, some nights I let my mind wander and imagined what could have been, though I only let myself go so far before pulling myself back and shutting those thoughts out. I couldn't let myself go there too much, the hurt was still there, and I didn't want to dwell for fear of plunging straight back into the despair of it all.

Kat suggested I set up a dating profile and get out there again, meet someone new. I was hesitant, it was the last thing I wanted to do. I told her I'd think about it, but in reality, I was scared of putting myself out there, of making myself vulnerable again. I didn't think I could trust anyone. I was so suspicious of everyone now, more so than ever before.

After much egging on I finally succumbed and got my dating profile up. I matched with a few people, all of whom seemed so egotistical or uninteresting that it put me off. I couldn't put it off much longer though, Kat was eager for me to at least go on one date with someone. I chose the guy that seemed the best of a bad bunch. "You're never gonna like anybody if you go in with that attitude" Kat told me. She was right, I needed to give it a proper chance. I set up a date with the guy, drinks that Friday at a nearby bar.

Honestly, I was dreading it, but thought it would calm Kat a little, and also what was the harm? Maybe it wouldn't be as bad as I had thought.

Friday came around quickly, much to my annoyance. I got ready for the date after work and waited until the last minute to leave the house. I walked to the bar and when I arrived, I didn't see him outside. I glanced inside and didn't see him in there either, but I was slightly early, so I stood outside and waited. I fucking hated waiting. I looked at my watch impatiently. If he wasn't here in 5 minutes I was going home, fuck this.

Just as I looked away from my watch, I saw someone walking towards me. I recognised him from his picture. He was a little taller than me, brown hair cut short, brown eyes, a boy next door face, not bad but not handsome.

"Hi!" he said enthusiastically.

"Hi!" I said with the same enthusiasm, "Mark?"

"Yeah" he said, "Miriam?"

"Yep!" I said, "let's go in?"

"Sure!" he said. We went inside and ordered drinks. He talked about sports for most of the next hour, his favourite team and what matches he was watching. I nodded politely and smiled along.

"So, what do you do?" he had finally asked me a question.

"Oh, I have a shop down the street here with a friend of mine" I said smiling, "I draw little postcards and she does cerami- he cut me off mid-sentence.

"Oh" he said, "you know what? A friend of mine has this postcard right that he got at one of the games and guess who he got it signed by?"

I shrugged my shoulders and took a sip of my drink, a famous harp player I thought sarcastically. I can't even remember what name he gave; I just know that I widened my eyes, faking surprise, and continued to nod politely. I had always had trouble getting out of conversations, I could never find the right moment to say oh I better go or excuse myself; it was so frustrating. Finally, a moment of silence, I could see he had almost finished his drink. "I'm just going to the bathroom" I said and walked away towards the ladies. I would spend a few minutes in there and then come back and make my excuses and leave. When I returned, he had bought me another drink and my heart sank. Nope, I said to myself, I'm not sitting here another second. Usually, I would have suffered through it but I had had it.

"I got you another" he said smiling.

"Oh thanks" I said, "but actually I have to leave, sorry about that, I have to get up super early."

"Oh" he said, looking disappointed.

"Yeah sorry, let's keep in touch" I said smiling, and put on my coat. I walked out and felt relieved. I hadn't forced myself to stay out of politeness, that was a first, standing up for myself, not doing something I didn't want to do. I felt a little proud. I started the walk home; it was only 9.15. I would have the whole evening to myself I thought and dreamed of getting into my pjs and curling up on the couch with a hot coffee.
Sure, the date hadn't gone well, but I was glad I went. I felt free, like I was back in control of my life, making my own choices. I took a deep breath in and looked up at the night sky, stars glistening brightly.

It was a clear night tonight I thought, I would be able to see the stars from bed. For the first time in a long time, I felt light.
I let my mind wander as I walked, how I would tell Kat about my date. She would get a kick out of it; it would be a good laugh. I smiled to myself as I neared my house.

Lost in thought, I reached my stairs and as I walked up I looked up at my door. My heart stopped. I froze. A figure was standing in front of my door, it was dark, and I didn't recognise who it was.

"Hi" I heard a man say. My mind frantically connected the dots until finally- Francesco.

Oh, fuck no, I thought.

"Hi" I said coldly, walking up the stairs and pushing past him, putting my key in the door. I didn't want to look at him.

"Can we talk?" he said. I felt my blood rising, my heart pounding in my ears.

"No" I said quickly, and as the door opened I threw myself inside, closing it behind me. I stood there, listening, trying to hear if he had walked away or if he was still there. I could only hear my own heartbeat throbbing in my head. My breathing was heavy and shaky, and I tried to slow it down. After a few minutes I still hadn't heard anything and walked down the hall to my bedroom, sitting on the bed, still listening for any sound.

I replayed what had just happened over and over, going over every detail. The tone of his voice sounded serious, when he had said hi it was a low high, his voice cracking. It was dark but I had seen his face briefly, his expression had been wary, he had seemed hesitant.
His dark coat, I remembered that coat. It all came flooding back to me, that day in the alley, his coat, his scent. No, I didn't want to remember this, I didn't want to think about this, it was over, he had hurt me so much. I wasn't going through that again and he didn't deserve anything more from me, but part of me had always wondered what had
really happened.
What had the "I'm sorry" been about? Why hadn't he contacted me ever again? Of course, I was curious, but knowing meant asking or at least talking to him, and I didn't want that, for him to have something I wanted. Suddenly the letterbox slit clunked against the door. I jumped, the noise startling me. I saw a white envelope on the floor. I stared at it for a few moments, not wanting to go directly to it in case he heard, in case it seemed like I was desperate to look.

I waited, motionless, staring at it, until finally I tiptoed down the hall towards it as quietly as possible. I reached down, still listening out for any noise outside, and picked up the envelope. I walked back to my bedroom and sat on the end of the bed. I looked at it, a plain white envelope. I felt nervous. I ripped it open and took out a single white folded page. I unfolded it and saw his handwriting all the way down the page. I started reading:

Miriam,

Firstly, I'm so sorry, with all my heart, sorry. I wanted to see you so that I could explain the last 3 months to you in person, but since you're reading this, I guess you've decided not to talk to me, and I completely understand. I would feel the same.

I want to make it clear that it was never my intention to leave you as I did. I was so happy, believe me, so so happy to be seeing you again, and I was so much looking forward to spending time together.

I told you once, during one of our conversations, that I had come out of a long-term relationship recently. I didn't elaborate because I didn't feel it was relevant that you know the whole story. I think I wanted to shut it out, and you made me want to shut it out because with you I felt happier than I had felt in such a long time. When things broke off with my ex, she had a hard time letting go of the relationship, which in turn made things harder for me. Her behaviour was erratic at the best of times and she wouldn't just let things be. After an incident where she turned up at my house in the middle of the night trying to break in, we decided she needed help. She got better and I gave her as much distance as I could until one night, we bumped into each other. We ended up drinking a lot, and then ended up sleeping together. This was a couple of months before I met you. I regretted it as soon as it had happened, and we agreed it was a once off. After that I didn't see her much. She had gotten on with her life and so had I.

Then I met you, and I fell in love. The day you were arriving, as I was leaving to make my way to the airport, she came to see me. She told me she was pregnant. At first, I didn't believe her, but she insisted it was true. She told me how she wanted us to be family.

When I told her I would support my child, but I couldn't be with her romantically, she became angry, telling me I didn't have a choice. She told me she knew I was seeing someone else, and if I didn't break it off and be with her, she would keep my child from me. I believed her. I was so deluded.

I decided it was best for you not to be part of any of this, you hadn't asked for this mess, and for shutting you out I'm sorry.

I spent the next couple of months trying to stay friendly with her, but it was hard, I missed you, but I needed things to be ok for my child. When she was far along enough, I insisted we go for a scan together and I was starting to have doubts.
She had shown me letters from her doctor, but I wanted to know for sure myself that this was really happening. After a lot of back and forth the truth came out. She wasn't pregnant and she never had been, it had all been a sick game to win me back, to get back to our old life. As soon as I found out I left, I don't want anything to do with her or her family. I changed my number. I booked my flights and I'm here Miriam, I'm here, please talk to me.
I love you; I miss you, I'm sorry with all my heart.
Francesco

Chapter 14

I sat in silence, trying to process what I had just read. Did I believe him? This was a crazy story. Still with the letter in my hand, I went into the kitchen and made a cup of coffee. I waited for it to finish, then sat down at the counter and read the letter again. I had thought we were over; I was still so hurt. He wrote that he loved me, it made my heart flip. It was bittersweet. Did I want to forgive him? I couldn't forget everything; it had been devastating. Why couldn't he have called at least or explained what was going on? I didn't know if I could get over that. What if something like that happened again?

I digested the contents of his letter all night. Reading and re reading it repeatedly. He had written his hotel details at the bottom, where he was staying, and a note to say I could go whenever I wanted to, or at least call him, his new number written underneath.

I didn't know what to do. I didn't want to make a fool of myself again, to be made a fool of, to be taken advantage of. What if he wasn't telling the truth? How gullible would that make me? I tossed and turned all night and when the morning sun shone through my window, I saw his letter beside me. In the light of day, it seemed clearer to me.

I wanted to talk to him, at least let him explain everything in person. I needed to see him so I could judge for myself if he was being truthful and if this was all genuine. I showered and got ready while I let my decision sink in. It felt right. I messaged him and for a moment I thought, he was going to think he had won, that I had given in. I typed my message; I could come see him now at his hotel.   I finished getting dressed and saw he had replied: Thank you Miriam, thank you for letting me explain, I'll be in the lobby waiting for you.

I gathered my things and walked out the door, apprehensive. No matter what, I would always second guess myself. Part of me was excited to see him, to pick up where things had left off, but I knew I couldn't let myself do that. I needed to be careful.

I walked to the hotel and took that time to think. I arrived and as I walked inside towards the lobby, that familiar smell sent a jolt through me as flashes of memories of our time together here reeled through my mind. Suddenly I saw him, sitting at a table alone at the back. He was looking down at the table and it gave me a moment to compose myself as I walked towards him. I had seen him yesterday, but it had been dark, now I could see all of him. I drank him in, his strong shoulders, his presence, the light bouncing off his dark curls. I bowed my head, willing myself to remember all the heartache, willing myself to hate him. I approached his table and looked up; our eyes met. His deep dark brown eyes and soft dark lashes, his soft face. My heart skipped a beat. He smiled, but it didn't reach his eyes, he looked sad. For a split second I wanted to hold him, to comfort him.

"Hi" he said, as I sat down. "Thanks for coming".

"Hi" I said, trying to sound strong and determined.

He got a staff members attention and ordered us both coffees. As we waited for them to arrive, he asked if I had read his letter. Obviously, I had if I was here, but I could understand him, being a little lost for words and not knowing where to start.

"I read the letter" I said.

I didn't want to say anything more, I wanted him to fill the silence, I was here to listen. I didn't owe him a conversation. Our coffees arrived.

"What are you thinking?" he asked.

"Well, I don't know" I said, "it's a bit of a crazy story". I looked down and shifted in my seat, wanting to seem detached.

"It is" he said, "and again I'm so sorry" I nodded and sipped my coffee.

He started talking about what had happened as I listened. It was exactly as he had written in the letter, the same story but with more detail as he retold it. He seemed lost and confused. When he spoke of the pregnancy I could see pain in his eyes, I could see that it had hurt him deeply. He had wanted to care for his child, to be a part of its life, but the situation was toxic. He looked as if he had had a heavy weight on his shoulders for a long time, he looked battle scarred. As he recounted his story, I looked at him and listened, feeling everything he was feeling. His eyes didn't lie, he was telling the truth. When he spoke of how he had found out it had all been a lie, I saw a flash of hurt across his face. He bowed his head; I think not to show it.
He said he had never felt so betrayed in his life, that he had felt things he never wanted to feel again. His pain for thinking he was going to become a father and then losing all of that in a split moment. At the same time, he had felt relieved that he wouldn't be bringing a child into this toxic mess, it wasn't right. I understood him. He spoke of his hurt at having to let me go, thinking he was doing the right thing for me. That I deserved better. I felt such compassion for him. He had done what he thought he had to at the time. He said I was the first person he wanted to see after everything blew up.

I asked him what his plans were now and for the first time since we started the conversation, he laughed out loud and said he didn't know. It lightened the mood and I smiled. It felt good to see him laugh, with his eyes too. I had felt elated when he talked about wanting to see me first after everything, and that he had missed me as much as he said he did. I felt the butterflies in my stomach returning. I wanted to hold him; I wanted him to hold me. I stopped myself, I didn't want to be too forgiving too quickly. I kept thinking that if all this was just some big lie, then I would be a real sucker. I couldn't trust him fully yet. But when he looked at me, I could feel myself drifting into him.

We talked and talked. I told him how my side of things had been, how hurt I had been. He reached out to me and placed his hand on my arm to comfort me. "I'm so sorry" he said, "truly". His touch sent a bolt through me and in that moment, I wanted him so much. I willed myself to push those thoughts aside as we continued talking. We had stayed so long that we decided to grab some lunch in their restaurant. Once we had moved on from what had happened and the conversation became lighter, we found each other again.
Talking with each other like we had done before all of this mess, laughing, enjoying each other's company. It felt freeing. We ordered some wine with our food and before I realised it, we had ordered a second bottle. The more we drank, the more we laughed, and the more comfortable we were, like us again. We stayed so long chatting that the waiters started setting up for dinner service and couldn't clear our table. They were giving us looks as they passed us, not wanting to ask us to leave.

We eventually paid and left. We walked out of the restaurant and into the corridor towards the lobby. I would get a taxi home I thought, I could feel myself a little unstable on my feet, this wine had really gone to my head. The whole time we had been talking I had been fantasising about kissing him, but I had stopped myself. I would get a taxi and get out of there. Just go home and replay the afternoon in my head.

Suddenly he stopped. I turned to him and stopped walking too. "What is it?" I said.

He looked at me and didn't reply. "Is everything ok?" I said.

He stepped towards me and reached his hand out. He brushed the hair away from my face. I looked up at him, and in that second, wished him to kiss me. My gaze fell to his lips. He came closer to me, his chest almost touching mine.
My heart was thumping.
He cupped my face with his hand and grazed my lips with his thumb. He moved his face towards mine and as I closed my eyes I felt his lips on mine, his soft lips, his soft beard brushing against my skin. It was as if no time had passed, he had made me feel the same intoxicating surrendering desire as he always had. I stopped thinking. He pressed his
lips against mine, softly, slowly, then he broke away. I opened my eyes.

"I missed you so much" he whispered. He moved close to me and found my lips with his a second time. I closed my eyes and let myself drift away, letting him take me. His tongue finding mine, I reached my hands to the back of his neck, my fingers combing through his hair. I had missed this; I had missed him. Suddenly my mind was brought back into the room as I heard someone shuffling past. I broke away from him to see people walking up and down the corridor looking embarrassed. Maybe this wasn't the best place for this I said, and we laughed. "You're right" he said, "come to my room".
He looked at me and smiled. "Please" he said, and I couldn't resist.
He took my hand and led me to the elevator, almost sprinting. Both of us laughed as we headed inside and as the door closed, he pulled me against him. Sweeping my hair off my shoulder, he kissed my neck. It felt so soft, God I was getting turned on, remembering how his mouth had felt on my body. The doors opened and he took my hand once more and led me down the hallway to the room door. He grabbed the card from his back pocket and slid it into the slot and out again.
The door buzzed and clicked open. He led me inside. It was dark, the curtains must be closed I thought. As the door shut behind us, he turned around, bent down and grabbed me, lifting me up into his arms. Before I had time to ask what he was doing he sat me down on the desk against the wall, across from the bed.

Spreading my legs, he came close to me so that our bodies touched, I could feel his hips pressing against my thighs. He kissed me hard, more urgently than before, our wet lips, our tongues finding each other's again. He hooked his hands under my knees and lifted them against him, pulling me. My skirt fell to either side of my hips exposing my underwear. I wanted to feel his mouth on me, I wanted him inside me, my head was spinning. He slid his hand up my thigh and his touch made my body tingle. He broke free and moved his head to kiss my neck. God, his lips, his tongue. I placed my hands on his chest, wanting to feel him, to feel every part of him. I felt his fingers brush over my underwear, between my legs. I moaned softly. His hand moved back to my thigh and slid slowly up towards my pussy again. Suddenly he broke away and reaching for my hips he grabbed my underwear and slid it down and off my legs. Dropping to his knees, he firmly spread my legs wider, and holding them in place, I felt his mouth on me.

I moaned louder this time. His tongue caressing my clitoris, his lips kissing it. I placed one hand on the desk to steady myself and the other through his hair, tugging at his curls as I felt myself building, I was going to come. "Yes" I said breathlessly and opened my eyes, looking down at him between my legs as he looked up at me and continued kissing me, licking me, slowly, firmly. As our eyes met, I couldn't hold it any longer. "Ah!" I cried out as I came hard. I fucking loved this man. Catching my breath, he stood up, and I reached out grabbing the waist of his jeans. I unbuttoned them and he pulled them and his boxers down. My legs still spread, he pulled them towards him and guided himself inside me, thrusting hard. He cried out, his breath shaky, as he pushed himself all the way in. It felt so good, he felt so good. He moved in and out of me with a hunger, a desire, that turned me on like never before. He moaned loudly and stopped still, dropping his head on my shoulder and breathing hard. I wanted him again and again, my appetite insatiable for him.

He moved out of me and kissed my mouth, a deep kiss, as he cupped my face. He wrapped his arms around me and lifted me up against him, turned around, and laid me down on the bed, kissing me again deeply. Breaking away he moved his mouth towards my ear. "I want you to come again" he whispered, sending a lightning strike down through my body. He kissed my neck, and I could feel myself getting wet again. Fuck I thought, this fucking guy.

He grabbed my jumper and slid it up my body. Hooking his finger inside the cup of my bra he pulled it down exposing my breast. Cupping my breast, he pressed his mouth over my nipple and I could feel his tongue brushing against it, sucking, biting gently, sending ripples of pleasure through me. Oh god yes, I thought. As he softly bit my nipple again, I suddenly felt his fingers on my pussy. I cried out. I was going to come again; this was so intense.

I bit my lip, not wanting to moan at his every touch. His fingers caressed my clitoris as he cupped my other breast, moving the cup down and taking my nipple in his mouth. I felt his finger slide inside me, in and out, and back to my clitoris. I moaned. He continued moving his fingers in and out of me, massaging my clitoris. He moved his face to my neck. "Come for me" he whispered in my ear, and it was enough to send me over the edge. I gasped loudly and moaned as I came, lost in the moment, lost in him.

We held each other and dozed in and out of sleep, finally moving into the bed where we spent the night together. Fuzzy from the wine and sleepy from the intensity of our lovemaking, I didn't want to leave.

The next morning, I woke up first. It took me a few seconds to remember where I was, to remember last night. Francesco was still sleeping. I looked at him for a few moments, his soft eyelids and long lashes, he looked so peaceful. I decided to let him sleep and to make my way home, I wanted a shower and to be with myself and my thoughts.

I quietly rolled out of the bed and gathered my clothes, strewn about the floor. I wanted to leave him a note to say I had left but the light in the room was sombre, and I couldn't see any pad or pen on the desk. I dressed myself and tiptoed towards the door, hoping the sound of it opening wouldn't wake him. I walked out and gently closed the door behind me. I made my way out of the hotel and into the strong daylight, I hadn't even checked the time.
8.15.
As I walked home, I thought about our night together, about our meeting, about the story he had told me. I believed him but part of me thought it was too crazy. I didn't want to be hurt again. Flashes of his kiss, the room, the sex, took over my mind.

He was the first man that focused on my pleasure, making me come as a priority, and also the first that understood that chances are I wouldn't be able to come from penetration alone.

In all my previous relationships, despite me making it clear I wouldn't be able to orgasm from just that, not one had concerned himself with my pleasure. Sure, they would do other things once in a while, but that was it. My satisfaction was never a focus, it was always an occasional occurrence, a treat almost. If he happened to be in the mood to do something extra then great for me, otherwise it was always straight intercourse. Don't get me wrong, I loved the intimacy, and it turned me on – but I just couldn't reach orgasm with it alone. When I had started discovering sex in my younger years, I always wondered if there was something wrong with me. In movies, the media, everywhere, the women always climaxed during sex. I didn't understand what I was doing wrong. As I got older, I quickly realised that I wasn't alone. In fact, this was the case with the majority of women. I couldn't believe it. I was relieved that it was something common, but it made me even more confused. Why were women being portrayed as having these crazy orgasms from intercourse alone when the majority don't?

The result was that now with Francesco I was surprised. Not only did he focus on me at first, but he was doing it every time. I almost felt a little guilty, like I was wasting his time.

I hoped that he wasn't making an effort to do it despite not wanting to. I had to shrug those feelings off. I remembered how he had looked, how excited it had made him to pleasure me, he liked it.
That's how it should be I thought, that's how it should have always been. I was angry at myself for having accepted anything less for such a long time. Fuck that. I was sexually satisfied for the first time in ... well for the first time in my life, and I was in my mid-thirties.

I arrived home and hopped into the shower. Washing him off my body, I missed him already. I got dressed and sent him a message telling him I had gone home to shower and hadn't wanted to wake him. He replied almost straight away saying that when he saw I had left he had gotten scared, thinking I had left for good. He asked if I wanted to do something with him that day. I said I would like that, and as it was a nice day I suggested going for a drive to the country. There were spectacular views not far from here, deserted spots. He had rented a car, so he offered to come pick me up in an hour.

Chapter 15

I felt excited to be spending a whole day with him, it was a change of scenery. I would ask him more questions about what had happened with his ex and see if I could spot any discrepancies. I didn't want to be led on, I wanted to know for sure he was telling the truth, that he really did love me as I loved him. I changed my outfit now that I was going out, it was a sunny day, so I opted for flowery flowy dress. I felt so feminine, so beautiful for the first time in a long time. He picked me up an hour later. "You look beautiful" he said as I sat into his car. "Thanks" I said, and he leaned over and kissed me, lingering for a few moments. My heart instantly in mouth, I briefly thought about fucking him right then and there. I reigned myself in and broke free from him.
With butterflies in my stomach, we drove off.

It was strange being in the car with him, it felt like we were a proper couple. Him driving and me beside, people could see us together and I felt pride that I was with this handsome man. We drove and drove into the country, the wilderness. The rocky landscape and green fields, and then through areas of forest thick with trees, rivers and lone sheep. The weather changing from sunny to dark stormy clouds to sunny again. We decided to grab some food and drive some more to find a nice spot to sit and eat. Sandwiches and drinks in hand, we drove until we found a rocky area overlooking a river, beside it a wooded area.

What a stunning view. We began to eat, and he stopped to take out his camera. It was the first time I had seen him with it. Up until now I had seen his pictures, but never him in action. He got out of the car, excusing himself, as the light outside was perfect to take a few shots. I stared at him, the camera against his face, his left hand adjusting the lens. How talented he was, I thought.

 I suddenly remembered the torn-up photo, the one I had ripped to shreds when I had gotten home from Sicily. I hadn't told him I had done that. Maybe I could replace it with one from today's set of shots, one from the present and not the past.

Lost in thought, I suddenly realised the camera was pointed in my direction. "Oh no!" I said, and covered my face with my hands, laughing. He walked towards the car still pointing it at me, as I tried to hide myself even more. I looked so bad in photos. I didn't care how talented someone was, it wasn't possible to take a good one of me. As he got back into the car, he put down the camera.

"Don't take photos of me" I said.

"Why not?" he said, "You're beautiful".

"No" I said, "I look awful in photos".

"I doubt that" he said. He laughed and said "Ok, I'll get you another time". He leaned over and with both of his hands cupped my face and kissed me. It felt soft against my lips, and I felt enveloped by him in an instant. He broke free and suggested we go for a walk. I agreed, it would give us time to talk. I hadn't had the courage or hadn't felt the right moment to bring up his ex in the car. We got out and started walking through the field, trees all around us. The sound of the river near us was calming, the sun on my skin and him beside me gave me peace and I felt excitement for things to come. I was happy.
We walked close to each other, sometimes briefly touching as we navigated the uneven terrain, which only heightened my desire for him. Being with him in a different environment was thrilling, like a snapshot of what our life would look like if things developed further and we ended up staying together. I was getting ahead of myself I thought, that was what had gotten me into this mess to begin with.

As we walked slowly, we talked and laughed. I loved talking with him, he could be so funny. His jokes and the way he described things, sometimes he was funny without even meaning to be. Suddenly he grabbed my hand and twirled me to him. Pressing himself against me he kissed me, more passionately this time, deepening the kiss. I could feel his hunger and it turned me on instantly. With his hands on my waist, he walked me backwards. Before I could ask what, he was doing I felt something hard against my back, I was against a tree.

He pushed his body against mine, pressing me harder against the rough bark and kissed me again. I could feel him over the material of my light dress. I felt his hand reach underneath my dress, between my legs. He broke free from the kiss and whispered, "open your legs". It sent a jolt through me. I parted my legs without thinking and as his fingers moved, caressing me over my underwear, I suddenly realized we were outside. Barely able to speak I said, "wait we're outside, anybody could come past and see us". He didn't reply and continued caressing me, rubbing me over my underwear. "What if someone comes" I said again, willing him not to stop. "Do you want me to stop" he whispered, and with that his fingers travelled inside my underwear, caressing me softly. I let out a quiet moan. No" I said, breathless. I lost myself, my eyes half closed, I let myself forget where we were.

"You drive me crazy" he whispered, as he slid a finger inside me. "Oh" I cried out, it felt so good, he felt so good. I wanted to reach out to him too, but I couldn't move, he had me pinned. He kissed me and his lips moved to my neck. His other hand slid over my chest and up to the strap of my dress, sliding it off my shoulder. It fell, exposing my breast. He kissed my shoulder, and his hand cupped my breast, the intensity of his touch felt too much to handle. I was going to come, he grazed his thumb over my hard nipple as he continued to caress me, sliding his finger in and out of me slowly moving to my clitoris and back. Suddenly he moved his head and placed my nipple in his mouth, licking it. As he gently sucked, I couldn't take it any longer and came, exploded. I cried out, unable to keep myself quiet. I felt him tug my underwear down and in one swift motion he twirled me around and pushed me up against the bark. Still breathless, I waited and heard him unbuckle his belt. He grabbed my waist and pulled my ass towards him. I felt his hard cock against my wet pussy as he pushed himself inside of me firmly. It felt so good. He moaned quietly and reached his hands to my breasts as he pulled out and pushed himself back in again, hard. "Fuck" he said as he thrust harder and harder inside of me. He lifted my skirt higher and fucked me harder and harder. Suddenly he stopped and cried out, breathing heavily. We didn't move for a few moments. "I couldn't help myself "he said smiling as I turned around to face him. We kissed. That had been so hot I thought, I had never done it outside like that before. I had always been so self-conscious but with him I didn't even care.

We drove back a little later, talking the whole way. I remembered I had work the next day but I didn't want to get back to reality, to be outside this bubble. I also hadn't told Kat about the letter, his return, none of it- so it really was a bubble. I was afraid she would tell me not to trust him and that I was better of without him.
She was probably right, but I couldn't get enough. He had no set departure date, although I knew he couldn't stay here forever. He hadn't told me about what his plan was. For now he was taking a break, he was here and that was as far as he had thought things through. I would spend that evening with him I thought, convincing myself it was the only logical thing to do, he was here after all. I would talk to Kat tomorrow, maybe take some time off. Take time off I thought, I was getting ahead of myself again. Sure, I was having the best sex of my life and he had told me he loved me, but was it real? Could we have an actual relationship? I needed to talk to him about it. What if he didn't want that? I would be crushed all over again.

We got back to his hotel and after some time in his room, fucking of course, we went out for dinner. I tried my hardest to bring up the subject of the future and what he wanted, but all I could think was what if he said he wasn't interested. That would ruin everything, well for me anyway. I would talk to him tomorrow, next time. We spent our evening eating and drinking, talking and fucking. Laying on his bed, he opened up about his past relationship and I appreciated that. I appreciated him being vulnerable with me, it made me feel secure. We finally dozed off.

The next morning, I decided to wake up a little earlier so that I could go home and get ready there, not wanting to wear the same clothes to work all day. His scent was on them and it would distract me too much.

He woke up as I rolled out of the bed and tried to drag me back in. What I would have done to stay the whole day with him in bed, our bodies sparking off one another's. I pried myself away and we agreed to make plans later. I walked briskly home, showered and dressed, and made my way to the shop.

When I arrived Kat was already inside, I went in and she took one look at me and said, "what's happened?" Damn. I had tried to act as normal as possible, but she knew me so well, I could never hide anything from her.

"Ok" I said, "You're not gonna believe this, don't be angry, hear me out, ok?"

"Okaaay" she said apprehensively – "Wait, he back isn't he".

"Yes" I said, "But hear me out".

She rolled her eyes. "I hope you told him to fuck off" she said.

"So, remember when I had that date the other night?" I said.

"Yeah" she said, "How did it go by the way?"

"Awful" I said, "He talked about football nonstop".

"Right" she said.

"So, I cut the date short, I got back to my place, and Francesco was there on my doorstep" I said.

"Mmh mmh" she said sarcastically.

"So, he asked if we could talk and I said no and went inside" I said.

"Ok good" she said, I hope that was the end of that". I paused.

"Of course, it wasn't" she said, "go on what happened".

"Ok so I got inside, and he put a letter under the door" I said.

"A letter?" she said, surprised.

"I know right?" I said, "so I get this letter and in it is this full explanation of what had happened, and why he didn't show in Sicily and why he hasn't been in contact since".

"Was he abducted by aliens?" she asked, "cause that would be the only explanation I would accept at this point".

"No" I said, "So it turns out his ex is a bit off, she never really accepted that they were over, and she had some problems".

"Riiight" she said, "Go on".

"So, the day I arrived in Italy, she shows up at his place and tells him she's pregnant with his kid and she wants to be with him" I said.

Kat said nothing but her jaw dropped.

"So" I continued, "he tells her he doesn't want to be with her but he'll take care of his child. I can only guess that meanwhile I'm on a plane about to land. So, she flips out and tells him that she knows he's being seeing someone else, and if he doesn't break it off with me and be with her, she's not going to let him be a part of its life".

I took a breath.

"So" I said, "he feels trapped and there's nothing he can do about the situation, and not wanting to drag me into it, he doesn't tell me what's happened. By that point I've already landed and he's not going anywhere".

"Ok" she said, "hold up, this story is crazy. For the record, do you believe this?"

"Let me finish" I said, "There's more".

"Ok, go on" she said.

"So" I said, "time passes, and he finally finds out that she was never pregnant, and it was all some sort of scam to force him into being with her. He's devastated obviously and hurt. He changed his number, and he came here to find me so he could explain".

Kat said nothing.

"That's it" I said.

Kat still said nothing.

"Say something" I said.

"I'm processing all this" she said. "So just to be clear, before I say anything about this, I'm guessing you ended up meeting up with him and you've been with him since?"

"I have" I said, looking guilty.

"Right" she said.

After a long pause she finally spoke.
"Ok here's how I see it" she said, "That story is crazy, like as crazy as being abducted by aliens, and if it were me, I wouldn't buy it. I know it's not what you want to hear, but happily ever afters don't happen in real life Miriam, it sounds too good to be true. So, he couldn't even send you a text? Because he didn't want to drag you into it? Please"
"I know" I said, "I thought the same but honestly Kat, he was so genuine when he spoke about it, I could see he was telling the truth, plus he's here now indefinitely".

"Ok, but what's your plan?" she said, "Are you guys an item now? Is he staying here for good? Is the ex out of the picture for good? How much do you really know about him?"

"I don't know about the ex" I said, "it sounds like she is, and I haven't spoken to him about any future plans yet, we've only just reconnected. I didn't want to bring it up straight away".

"I don't know about this Mims" she said as she shook her head.

"I know I know" I said, "I'm gonna be careful, I promise".

"You'd better be" she said, "because I don't buy it, and if that story is true and he's made it back to you in true prince charming fashion then great, true love lives, but until we know for sure what the deal is I don't want to see you hurt again, please don't rush into it".

"I won't" I said, "I promise I won't, I half believe him, and half don't, I'm being cautious".
"Ok" she said, "I'm not sure how cautious you can really be with your legs in the air though".
She laughed and so did I, it broke the tension and I felt relieved that she knew what was going on, that she was looking out for me.

We joked around all day, and it was a welcome distraction, because otherwise I would have been thinking about him, about the sex and about his face all day long. I made plans with him to meet that evening at my place for dinner, he wanted to cook for me. I told Kat.

"Aww" she said, "so romantic. What else does he do? Does he have a magic carpet too?" We laughed and laughed.

I was buzzing when I left the shop for the evening, looking forward to getting home, to seeing him. I practically sprinted home, he was coming by soon. I gave the place a quick tidy up and he arrived on time, bag full of ingredients in one arm and a bottle of wine in the other. He got to work in the kitchen making pasta, a carbonara. I loved seeing him cook, there was something so sexy about a man cooking. I thought about Lorenzo and how he was the last man to cook in this kitchen. I thought about how awful it would be if he happened to come by at this moment, seeing another man here with me.

I had spoken to Lorenzo recently and he seemed to have moved on, but he wasn't overly friendly which I understood. I missed him, having him around the house, sharing my news with him, being a part of each other's lives and decisions. I wondered if I had done the right thing, and then I remembered how our relationship had been, the bad sides, the practically non-existent sex life, the loneliness. No relationship was ever going to be perfect though, and sometimes I felt as if I was chasing something that didn't exist. With Francesco we had a great sexual connection, but in the long run would he be there for me? I wanted to follow my heart, and I had done that at the expense of someone else. I hoped it hadn't all been for nothing.

The meal was delicious, I could get used to this I thought. We finished the wine and opened another bottle. I was going to regret this in the morning. Halfway through the second bottle, I gathered my Dutch courage and asked him straight out.

"What are your plans now?" I said, "What's going on with us?". I looked down and took a sip of wine, afraid of seeing his reaction.

"Well," he said, "for now I don't have any plans, I know I'll have to go back to Italy soon" .

I nodded. "Mmh mmh" I said.

"And for us" he said, "well I don't know that either. I don't have any plans, but I know I want to be with you, if you want to be with me?"

"I do of course" I said, relieved.

"I don't know how this is gonna work" he said, "I mean, you live here, and I live there, I know this is all a bit crazy, and with everything that happened I understand that it's a weird situation".

"It is" I agreed, "I guess we can play it by ear?"

"I think we can do that" he said smiling, and he raised his glass. I clinked mine against his and we both took a sip.

Before I knew it, it was already 1 in the morning. I cringed as I thought about getting up for work the next day. As I cleared the plates and placed them in the sink, he came up behind me, wrapped his arms around me and said "come to bed, its late, we'll do them tomorrow".

Being in his arms, I couldn't resist, and we made our way to the bedroom where he proceeded to undress me, kissing me as he went. I did the same to him and was turned on at the sight of his body, his chest, his arms.

I kissed his stomach as I unbuckled his belt, looking up at him and looking to ignite that fire on his eyes, that hunger. I pulled his jeans down and saw that he was hard through his boxers. I excited him, I liked that. I pulled down his boxers, kissing him again. His cock hard in front me, I wanted him. Kissing the tip at first and then licking slowly, I pushed him into my mouth. He felt smooth and warm. I sucked him and he moaned quietly, running his fingers through my hair, moving it away from my face. Having him in my mouth turned me on even more. I sucked and licked, like I couldn't get enough of him. Suddenly he whispered, " touch yourself for me". I looked up at him and saw the fire in his eyes. Feeling bold and loose from the
wine, I indulged him and let myself go. I wasn't self conscious   like I always had been. Keeping eye contact, I reached down between my legs, I felt wet. My fingers caressed my clitoris and I moaned softly. Licking and sucking him and being vulnerable in front of him, touching myself, felt good. He was fixated on me, he liked watching me. "You feel so good" he whispered as he moaned again. Fuck this was hot I thought, he's so hot. I sucked him harder as I felt myself building, I was going to come soon. Suddenly he cried out. He came hard in my mouth. I felt in control of him, I liked it. Breathing heavily he pulled out of me and lifted me to the bed. Grabbing my legs and lifting them up, then parting them, he placed his mouth on my pussy and kissed and sucked me as I came. My body trembling from the explosion. That had been intense, it was always intense with him.

We crawled into bed and fell asleep quickly in each other's arms. Before I drifted to sleep, I thought how lucky I was to have met him, again. Surely there had to be a catch as Kat had said, it was too good to be true.

When the alarm rang the next morning, I opened my eyes and the hangover instantly hit me. I shouldn't have drunk so much, I felt like I was still drunk. I groaned and hit the snooze. I must have fallen asleep again because when it rang a second time it had woken me from a deep sleep. I turned it off and rolled out of bed. Francesco opened his eyes.

"I'm going to take a shower" I said, and he nodded.

Bleary eyed, I stumbled into the bathroom and switched on the light. It hurt my eyes. I took a shower I felt a little better afterwards, getting dressed and ready. When I walked out into the kitchen, Francesco was at the sink doing the dishes.

"There's a coffee for you on the counter" he said. I was pleasantly surprised.

"Oh thanks" I said, "but you don't have to do the dishes, honestly leave them I'll do them later."

"I'm done anyway" he said, "I'll have a coffee with you".

We drank our cups together and the thought of leaving him and going to work filled me with dread.

"What if I took some time off?" I said.

"That would be great" he said, "I want more time with you". He kissed me. I was on cloud nine. It couldn't get any better than this I thought.
"I'll sort something out" I said.

He got dressed and we left together, he walked me to work. I missed him already and couldn't wait to see him after work.

"Talk to you later" he said, as we arrived at the shop.

We kissed goodbye and I went inside. Kat glanced up at me, "good night?" she asked.

"It was" I said, grinning.

"Jeez, this guy" she said, rolling her eyes. I laughed. Honestly despite the hangover I was so smitten I couldn't have not been in a good mood. The day passed slowly, as it always did when I was looking forward to something afterwards. We had made plans to meet up later that evening for dinner.

I told Kat I would be taking a few days off and she agreed it was ok, although reluctantly. At 6 on the dot, I raced out of the shop, rushing home so that I could get ready. I had butterflies in my stomach.

As I was picking out my outfit, my phone pinged. I picked it up, assuming it was a text from Kat. It was from him, I opened it and my heart sank as I read it: There's been an emergency, I need to fly back tonight, I'll be back as soon as possible, I'm so sorry.

Oh no no no no, this was not happening again. What emergency? I replied back: Is everything Ok? and waited for him to reply. I hoped it wasn't bad news, but I was so suspicious of everything now. He replied: I'll explain everything to you as soon as I can.

This was NOT happening again. Without thinking, I grabbed my coat and keys and headed out the door. I would catch him at his hotel, I wasn't going to let him leave without a proper explanation.

I flagged a taxi and headed straight there. Inside the hotel, I knew his room number by heart and hurriedly made my way up. I banged on the door. No response. I moved my ear close to the door to listen but couldn't hear anything. I banged on the door again and after a moment it clicked open. There he was in front of me, white as a sheet. He looked scared out of his mind. I instantly forgot my own anger and asked him what was wrong. I followed him inside and saw an open suitcase on the bed, clothes scattered everywhere, and his laptop open to the airline page on his desk. At least he was telling the truth about that I thought. Part of me had expected to catch him in a lie. Throwing his clothes in the suitcase and briskly walking around the room collecting items, throwing them in, he seemed in a hurry.

"What time is your flight?" I asked.

He seemed so focused, he didn't hear me, like he had too much on his mind. Anxious to know what had happened and what was going on, I asked him again, louder this time.
"What time is your flight?"

What? He said "Oh, it's at 3 in the morning. I'll drive up as soon as I'm ready and return the car". He rushed around the room grabbing what he could to throw inside the suitcase.

"What happened? What's going on?" I asked. He didn't say anything.

"Tell me" I said again, "Is everything ok? What's happened?"

"I can't talk about it now" he said, sounding annoyed. I felt out of place suddenly in his room, as if I was in a stranger's room and had overstayed my welcome. I knew if went home like this I would obsess about what the reason could be and imagine the worst. I couldn't leave without an answer, I owed myself that much.

"Look" I said sternly, raising my voice, "I'm going to leave, but you're going to tell me what's going on first". He looked up at me briefly and said nothing.

"I'm not leaving until you tell me" I said. He stopped what he was doing and took a breath in.

"Look" he said, "there's nothing for you to worry about, there's something going on with my ex and she might be in trouble. I just need to go and sort things out".

The ex I thought, here we go again. I repressed the urge to roll my eyes. What trouble could she be in that required him to be there?

"What trouble? I asked.

"Just trouble, ok?" he said, "I'll explain everything to you when I get there".

"But why do you need to go?" I asked.

"Because I just do" he said raising his voice. "Look, the police are involved, they need me to speak with them and it won't take long. I'll come back as soon as I've spoken with them, and I'll only be gone a couple of days at most, ok?"

He walked over to me and cupped my face in his hands. "Everything's ok" he said, looking into my eyes, "don't worry please".
He kissed me softly and for a moment the panic was over, like it had never been there. I calmed down, it seemed he did too, he wasn't as frantic with the packing as before, making his way to the bathroom to collect the rest of things.

"I'm going to go then" I said, "I'll leave you to pack".

"Ok" he said, coming out of the bathroom. "I'll call you as soon as I've arrived there, ok?"

"Ok" I said, walking towards the door.

"I love you" he said, as he came towards me. He kissed me again.

"I love you too" I said and walked out the door.

Outside the hotel I grabbed a taxi back home, I didn't feel like walking. I was reeling, it had all happened so fast. So many questions running through my mind – the police? What trouble could she be in if the police was involved? If she was as crazy as he had described, God knows what she could be involved in.

He had been so distracted then, so snappy with me. I had never seen him like that. He must be worried I thought, after everything he'd been through with her, I'm sure he cared about her to some degree. He must not have a choice but to go if the police are involved, I thought. Strangely that made me feel a bit better about everything, that it hadn't been his choice to go. He had been summoned; it was out of his hands. I hoped I would get more answers from him later and that he would tell me the full story. His face had been so pale when he had answered the door, he had looked scared – why had he not wanted to tell me what the trouble was? He was rushing I thought, probably in shock, he wasn't in any state to answer questions.

Chapter 16

I kept my phone with me all night beside me in bed, waiting for a message, but nothing came. When I woke up the next morning, I messaged him. Everything ok? I wrote. He should have arrived by now. I got up and tried to keep myself busy, cleaning the house, making lunch. Still nothing from him. He must be busy.
Still though a message couldn't be that hard. I was frustrated. How could he have made me feel like I was the only person in the world one minute, and like I wasn't anybody important the next. I wish I just knew what was going on.

My phone rang in the late afternoon. I saw it was him and rushed to answer it.

"Hello?" I said.

"Hi amore" he said. He sounded tired.

"How are you? Is everything ok?" I asked, for what felt like the thousandth time.

He sighed. "Yes, everything's ok. I arrived earlier and I've been at the police station all afternoon". The line was crackly.

"What happened? Will you have to go back to see them again?" I said.

"What?" he said, the line cutting in and out. I repeated myself.
"Yes, I'll go back tomorrow morning" he said. "It's my ex, Martina, they can't find her". The line crackled again. Had I heard that right?

"What?" I said, "They can't find her? What do you mean they can't find her?"

"She's missing" he said, "Nobody's seen her or been able to reach her and they think she might be in trouble. I have to help anyway I can".

"Of course," I said, lost for words. She was missing. In trouble somewhere? It was only right that he helped I guessed.

"Do you have any idea where she might be, or what might have happened?" I said.

"No" he said, "I haven't seen her for over a week and since I changed my number, I haven't been in contact with her at all".
"Ok" I said, "and are you ok?". There was a pause.

"I'm tired" he said, "I just wanna go home and sleep. I'll talk to you later, ok?"

"Alright" I said, "take care of yourself, I hope there will be news soon".

"Thanks" he said, "Bye", and hung up.

His voice had sounded like his face had looked the night before. He must have been stressed, of course he was stressed.

He had cut off ties with her after how she treated him and now, he was dragged back into another drama. That's how it felt anyway.

Selfishly I thought about how something always got in the way of us. I just wanted to hug him and be with him, to tell him it would all be ok. After everything he had been through, now this. He didn't deserve this. Part of me hoped she had just moved somewhere else for good, so he could properly move on with his life.

I went back to work the next day and filled Kat in on the situation. She could hardly believe it. "I guess there really was an ex then" she said.

I heard from Francesco every night after that, he had stayed longer than he thought he would have. What was supposed to be a couple of days turned into one week and they still hadn't found her. He needed to stay close by in case the police needed him, he wasn't doing much except waiting and participating in the searches organised for her.

I felt so bad for him, for everyone.

I wondered what could have happened to her. I had gathered more details about the whole situation the more we talked. She had been supposed to go to her parents' house for dinner one night and had just never arrived. Her parents called the police straight away when she didn't answer her phone, and since she was in a fragile state of mind, they were worried she might have done something to herself, or that she had gotten confused and had gotten lost.

They were out of their mind with worry. Since Francesco had seen her before he came here, he had been asked to come in and answer some questions. Any details helped at this point. They had interviewed everyone she knew. We just had to wait I guessed, wait for news, wait for an update.

A week turned into two and I missed him like crazy. He said he missed me too and it was hard being apart. He was worried and sometimes distant. I couldn't begin to imagine what he was feeling.

He couldn't help but worry, and since their last interaction hadn't been the sweetest, he felt guilty about it. He kept wondering if their conflict had driven her to do something. I told him not to think like that and that this wasn't anyone's fault.

I kept up to date scrolling through the local news coverage online with the help of google translate: Case of missing woman, still searching, anyone with any information – no other updates.

By week three they were searching in the woods and in every river close to the area. It was clear they were searching for a body, although they still said it was a missing persons case. I guessed they were exploring every avenue they could. Francesco was still waiting there, still helping with the searches and still worried out of his mind.

"What if something happened to her?" he said one night. "I'm sure they'll find her" I said, trying to reassure him.

"I don't know" he said sighing, "where could she be? They should have found her by now".

"I know" I said, "but don't lose hope".

It was hard knowing what to say, how could I possibly comfort him? What could I possibly say to make it better? I thought about going to see him, and then thought better of it. He didn't need me there in the middle of all this, I would only be a nuisance. I quickly talked myself out of it. If he needed me, he knew he could ask me.

One morning, at the start of week 4, I got up and scrolled through the news feed while I had my coffee. As I refreshed it and scrolled down through the last updates, my heart sank. Body found, it read, in case of missing woman. Oh no I thought, they've found her dead. They had found her body in the river, not far from her parents' house. There wasn't any more information, but they described it as an accidental drowning. It looked like she either fell or threw herself in. God. I messaged Francesco: I've just seen the news, are you ok? He replied: No, but at least we have some answers now. I told him to let me know if he needed anything, I was here.

This was crazy I thought, I had known she was unstable from what Francesco had told me, but could she have really done this to herself?

For the next couple of days there wasn't any new information. The body had been taken in for an autopsy and Francesco had stuck around for the family, to be there for them. Anyone else would have left but he had stayed and put his life on hold for these people. I loved his kindness. The general consensus was that she had fallen in although nobody close to her wanted to believe that, which was understandable. The autopsy was going to take time, and as the days passed and everyone continued to wait, Francesco said he wasn't needed any longer. The family had thanked him for his help, but they felt he had done all he could for them and wanted him to get back to his life.

He called me one night and told me he had booked his flight to come back. I asked him if he was sure that's what he wanted to do, maybe he would want to be there when the results came out. He said it could take days for that and that there was nothing more he could do. He wasn't much help to anyone anymore. He wanted to see me and he wanted to leave and process everything. He wanted to distance himself and start mourning. I didn't know what version of him I would find when he returned. I had never seen him truly sad; he would be broken. I needed to prepare myself for that. He was due to arrive two days later. I offered to let him stay with me, but he said he didn't want to put me out, and he needed to have his space too. I understood. I decided to take some days off for when he was here, so I could be with him as much as I could, if he needed.

Kat was horrified by the whole thing and told me to take as much as I needed to be with him.

He arrived in the evening a couple of days later. I had invited him to come to mine. Once he had checked in at his hotel, he got a taxi over. I saw him arriving from the window. I felt excited, I couldn't wait to see him and to wrap my arms around him. It was so selfish of me I knew, in the midst of this horrible event.
He walked up to the door and knocked. I opened it and there he was. I scoured his face trying to read his expression, was he upset? Was he happy? He smiled but his eyes were sad. Poor thing, I thought as I went to hug him.

He held me tight. "It's soo good to see you" he said as he clung on.

"You too" I said and buried myself in his embrace. It was comforting to hold him, to be held. It felt as if part of me had been away and now was back in its place. We parted and he kissed me softly. I breathed him in, his scent, I had missed him.

He came inside and we ate. I had prepared something in advance in case he was hungry. As we ate, he told me how he felt like he was still in shock.

"Of course, you're still in shock" I said, "it's going to take time for this all to sink in. I'm so sorry for all this". He bowed his head and nodded. He wasn't very talkative, and I wasn't surprised, I had expected it. He looked tired. After we had eaten, we decided to go to bed. It had been a long day. We slipped in between the sheets and held each other, not saying a word, until we both fell asleep. It had been so bittersweet, I wished I could make his pain go away. I wished there was something I could have done.

The next morning, I woke up before he did. I wanted to let him sleep, he needed it. I tiptoed out of the room, closing the bedroom door quietly behind me, and went into the kitchen to make some coffee.

I checked the news out of habit even though I knew there wouldn't be any update. I scrolled down through the feed; they were still waiting for the autopsy results. I clicked the phone off and sipped my coffee, letting my mind wander. I thought about the night before, how down he had been. What could I do to cheer him up? Would he want to do anything today? I would let him sleep as long as possible, maybe I could head out to the shop and get some pastries for when he wakes up I thought. I took another sip of my coffee before grabbing my coat and purse. I slipped on my shoes and headed out, trying to make as little noise as I could. I walked to the shop 5 minutes away and got a couple of different pastries. I got back home and slipped inside, listening out for any noise that might tell me he was awake. It seemed he wasn't. I laid the pastries out on a plate and made myself another coffee. I sat back down, letting my mind wander again.

Suddenly I heard shuffling coming from the bedroom. He must be waking up I thought. I listened and finally heard the bedroom door opening. I looked down the hall and saw his silhouette in the doorway.

"Hi" I said. He started walking down the hall towards me. "Hi" he said, "Why didn't you wake me?". I got up and went to the counter to prepare him a coffee.

"I wanted to let you sleep" I said as I switched on the coffee machine. I heard him come into the kitchen and walk towards me. Suddenly his arms were around me, hugging me from behind.

"Is that for me?" he asked. I assumed he was talking about the coffee.

"Yeah" I said, "you want one, right?"

"Of course," he said, as he rested his chin on my shoulder, "Thanks". He kissed my neck softly. I felt a rush and closed my eyes briefly at his touch. The machine whirred and with his arms still around me I suddenly saw his hand reach forward and touch the counter. As he pulled it away, there was a little blue velvet box sitting there.

"What's that?" I asked, surprised.

"It's for you" he said, still holding me. He kissed my neck again.

"For me?" I said, "What is it?"

"Open it" he said.

I knew what it looked like, but no, it couldn't be. It was probably a nice piece of jewellery, that was nice of him. I reached out and took the box, the velvet was soft between my fingers. I carefully lifted the stiff lid and as it popped open, there, shining in front of me, was the most beautiful diamond ring I had ever seen. Nobody had ever given me anything like this before, I couldn't believe what I was seeing. A ring?
My heart started to pound, was he going to ask me to marry him? Don't get ahead of yourself I thought, maybe it's just a nice ring. I stared at it, speechless.

"What do you think?" he said.

"Wow" I said, "it's beautiful".

"I couldn't help it" he said, "When I saw it, I knew, I knew it was meant for you".

"It's really beautiful" I said, not finding any other words.

"I hope you don't think I'm crazy" he said, "but I love you Miriam". "Will you marry me?" he whispered into my ear.

It sent a tingle through me. Oh my god I thought, this is actually happening, I love this man, and he's asking me to marry him, to be his wife. My mind was racing. I took the ring out of the box and looked at it.

"Oh my god" I said, "Yes, I will" I said and slid it onto my finger. I was surprised it fit, it fit perfectly. Somehow, I took it as a sign that I was doing the right thing. I turned around and kissed him.

"I love you" I said.

"I can't believe you're going to be my wife" he said smiling.

"I know, me neither" I said smiling back.

We kissed again. It meant so much more now, it was different. Our kiss deepened, our tongues finding each other at last. His soft lips, his soft beard against my face. My fingers found their way through his hair, his curls familiar, it felt like home.
I was already turned on, I wondered if he was too. Would he need time?

My question was answered almost immediately as his hands grabbed my waist and spun me around quickly. He pulled down my pants and underwear firmly. I gasped and heard his breath become heavier, as he pressed his body against mine. His hand reached down and without hesitation his fingers were between my legs, caressing me. I gasped again, he felt so good. I held on to the counter. The ring clinked on the marble top, and I noticed the unfamiliarity of it. I closed my eyes and parted my legs. He slid his finger in and out of me with ease, I was so wet already. His other hand cupped my breast over my top and then found its way underneath. His fingers traced over my nipple, pinching softly. I moaned.

He kissed my neck; I felt his bulge against my back as he pressed his body harder against me. I was going to come, his fingers caressing my clitoris, I felt myself building. I squeezed the counter and suddenly a thousand sparks escaped my body, pleasure soaring through me. My eyes still closed; I savoured the moment as my grip on the counter relaxed. His hands left me. I heard him pull his boxers down, then, his warm hard penis against my pussy. He guided himself inside me gently, and once inside, he firmly pressed himself against me. He pulled out of me slowly, agonisingly slowly, pleasure coursing through me once more. Suddenly he pushed inside of me again, hard. We both cried out. Again, he pulled out of me slowly, so slowly. I fought the urge to push him into me, I wanted him so badly. He lingered and then thrust again firmly. He pushed the hair away from my shoulder and kissed my neck as he continued slowly pulling out and firmly pushing in, until he cried out one last time and stilled. He buried his face in my shoulder, breathing rapidly. I turned around and wrapped my arms around him. He held me, our bodies pressed against each other. I was so happy in that moment I felt like my life was just beginning.

Chapter 17

Reeling from his proposal, we spent the next couple of days wandering around arm in arm, through the streets, sightseeing, eating, talking and laughing. I felt as though he was looking for anything to distract him, as we waited for any news about the autopsy findings. I tried not to bring it up and to keep jolly, secretly ecstatic about the ring I had on my finger and just loving being with him.

We should have been receiving news any day now, but I could tell that he was tense as the days passed. I guessed he was waiting for his closure. Although he seemed content with me, a part of him seemed closed off sometimes, as if waiting for a release. I wanted there to be news so that he could move on, or at least start to heal properly.

As we moved through the streets, I feigned interest in the sights, all the while relishing him, wanting him, thinking about being his wife, being his. We visited a market. It was full of people and excited chatter and laughter. I held on to him as we made our way through the crowds, wondering if I could stop time and stay in this moment. The sun was shining although it was cold, and it would be setting soon. The excitement of dusk, the unknown, of what the night ahead might bring. Dusk was always my favourite time of day, that change from day to night, like a new page.

"Do you like strawberries?" he said, jolting me out of my daydream.

"What? Err I do yeah, strawberries?" I said.

"Where were you?" he chuckled, "Yeah, strawberries, do you like them?"

"Of course," I said, laughing, "who doesn't like strawberries?!"

We were stopped at a stall selling fruits and vegetables, and there in front of us were the biggest strawberries I had ever seen.

"Juiciest ones you'll find!" said the man behind the stall as he grinned, "I'm proud of these ones!"

Francesco bought a couple of punnets, and the man bundled them into a brown paper bag.

"Can't wait to try these" Francesco said grinning. I saw a glint of playfulness in his eyes. We continued our tour of the market, and as we made our way out and started walking back home, dusk had fallen. We walked and walked.
"Your shop is coming up here, isn't it?" he said, "Could I have a proper tour?"

"You want a tour of my shop?" I said surprised, "But you've seen it before!"

"I know" he said, "but I mean, a proper tour. It's closed now, right? I can have a proper look".

"I don't know if I even have the keys on me" I said, rummaging inside my coat pocket. I pulled out my keyring and attached were various different keys, most of which I couldn't remember for where.

"There it is" I said, pinching the golden shop key. "Ok, I guess we can have a quick look if you really want to. I hope
Kat hasn't left it a mess!"

We approached the shop. I could tell Kat wasn't here, as the darkness inside the shop was visible through the windows. I clicked the door open and walked in, Francesco behind me, and closed the door behind him. The streetlights had come on outside, illuminating the shop in a low glow. I went to turn on the light, but Francesco grabbed my arm to stop me.

"No light" he said.
"But we can hardly see anything" I said, "So much for the tour!"

"Well, we can see out, but no one can see in" he said For a moment it hadn't clicked. What was he on about? He wanted a tour, now he wanted to look out the window. He slipped his hand around my waist and moved his face close to mine, almost touching my lips but not quite. I felt his breath against my skin, now I understood. He walked me backwards until I felt my back touch the cold wall. He pushed his body against mine, his face close again, his breath slightly faster and deeper, his lips almost touching mine. Outside the window to my left, people were walking up and down the street, oblivious to us in the dark. My heart beat faster. He parted his lips and pressed them against mine. His warm tongue found mine. My eyes closed. He stopped kissing me and moved his head beside mine. "You have such a pretty mouth" he whispered.

My heart skipped a beat as his whisper tingled in my ear. He kissed me again, more forcefully, pushing his tongue inside my mouth. He stopped again.
"I want to fuck it" he whispered. I was caught by surprise at how direct he was, how commanding. He faced me, locking eyes with me. His face was expressionless.
"Kneel" he said sternly, his face still expressionless and his eyes bright. I didn't think. His sudden authority over me stunned me, excited me. I sank to my knees and turned my face upwards to look at his. He reached for the buttons on his jeans and began to unbutton them. His eyes locked on mine, not looking away for a moment as I waited. He reached inside and pulled out his hard cock, holding it in his hand.
"Open your mouth" he said. I did as I was told and opened my mouth, waiting to taste him. I could feel myself getting wet. He placed the warm tip into my mouth, and my lips closed around it, my tongue caressing him. He pushed more inside my mouth, and more again until he was fully inside. Caressing him with my tongue, I moved my arms up to hold him close to me. He grabbed my arms before I could. "Keep your arms behind your back" he said, and I did as I was told, turned on by his authority, wanting to please him.
He pushed himself in and out of my mouth slowly. "Mmm" he whispered, "good girl". I felt my heart skip a beat again, he had never been like this with me before. I liked it. He reached out, grabbed a fistful of my hair and wrapped it around his hand, tightening it gently, giving him more control and giving me less. I liked it even more.

He softly moved my head in rhythm with him, my mouth taking him fully in and out. "Mmm" he whispered, "spread your knees". I moved my knees further apart. "More" he said, and I moved them as far as they would go, my long skirt draped over them. He continued rhythmically, in and out of my mouth. Show me how much you like me fucking your mouth" he whispered.

I reached for my skirt and gathered it up, holding it with one hand and reaching my other hand into my dripping wet underwear. My fingers found my clitoris and I moaned. "Mmm, good girl" he said, moving faster in and out of my mouth, moving my head and tightening his grip on my hair. I moaned again, my wet fingers rubbing my clitoris. "You're my dirty girl" he said and moaned, "mmm you like that, dirty girl?" He moved more forcefully now. I was ready to come. I groaned and came, hard.
He groaned as he came after me, breathing hard and fast. He closed his eyes.
He looked down at me and smiled as he tidied himself up. I smiled back as I gathered myself and stood up, my legs wobbly. Neither of us said anything, there was nothing to say. Wow.
We headed for the door and stepped out into the cold night air. We walked home hand in hand, not saying a word. I looked around at the people walking past and felt like I was in some sort of club, that I had a secret. When we reached the house, I jingled my keys, noticing for a second the golden shop key and almost blushing at the memory of what had just happened there. I turned the key in the door and opened it, going inside, feeling him behind me, wanting to look at him but feeling embarrassed to do so.

"Do you want something to eat? I said without meeting his gaze, the words cracking as they escaped me.

"Yes, I do" he said, "but I'm not finished with you yet".

My eyes betrayed me and sprang upwards to him, wide. Smiling, he reached down into the brown paper bag and pulled out a punnet of strawberries.

"Come" he said and reached out his hand. I took it and smiled suspiciously.
"What are you up to?" I said.
He didn't reply and led me to the bedroom, still holding the punnet. He led me to the bed and motioned for me to lay down. He put the punnet down and propped himself up beside me.
He kissed me slowly, his tongue in my mouth. He stopped and reached down behind him, taking a strawberry from its pack and holding it in front of me. Parting his lips, he opened his mouth slightly and placed the strawberry on his tongue, closing his lips around it, sucking it before pulling it out again. He held it against my lips. "Pretty mouth" he whispered, as he slowly brushed it against my top lip and across to my bottom lip. "Suck it" he whispered, as he pushed it into my mouth.
My lips closed around it and my tongue brushed its smooth and ragged surface. He pulled it out. Sliding my jumper up and yanking down my bra cups, exposing my breasts, he placed the wet strawberry on my nipple, circling it slowly. He moved to my other nipple, circling slowly once more. "You like that?" he whispered.
"Mmm" I whispered back. I closed my eyes and arched my back, dizzy.

His body moved down and as I opened my eyes; he lifted my knees. My skirt fell around my waist. He hooked my underwear with his fingers and peeled them down my legs and off me. I felt his breath against my pussy. Suddenly, I felt a sharp coldness. The coldness of the strawberry against my clitoris. Rubbing gently, circling. I looked down to see him staring at me. We locked eyes as he continued, the strawberry feeling foreign yet so sensual. I wanted to bite it, to taste it.

The coldness made its way from my clitoris downwards. I arched my back and moaned. He was teasing me, I wanted to explode. I felt the tip of the strawberry barely enter me, the sensation surprising me and teasing me further. My pussy throbbed, it felt hot, I wanted more. He stopped and lifted himself up over me. He held the strawberry to my mouth. "Suck it" he whispered, and I took it into my mouth, tasting it and me, watching how it excited him. "Bite it" he whispered.
I gave in and bit into the juicy fruit, its flavour exploding in my mouth. As he pulled it out the juice ran down the side of my face and without hesitation, his tongue was on my cheek, licking the sticky juice from my face, slowly licking it all up. We locked eyes and he took a bite of the strawberry, the juice running into his beard making his lips and chin wet. "Mmm" he whispered, as he moved himself back down, placing his head between my legs.

He pressed his wet mouth and chin into my pussy, his tongue licking me, the juice spreading all over me, his tongue licking it up. The taste of the strawberry still lingered in my mouth as I closed my eyes and gave in. As his tongue buried itself in me, I felt myself fall over the threshold and came hard. I moaned as he stood up, pulled his jeans and boxers down and quickly and forcefully thrust himself inside me, once, twice and then he came.

We laid together afterwards on the bed and fell asleep. I was exhausted, blissfully exhausted. I couldn't help but think I didn't deserve this, to be happy. It was too good to be true.
As I lay next to him and drifted to sleep, my thoughts turned to his ex. Please let there be news soon I hoped, then we could start planning our life together.

The next morning, I woke up to the sound of a distant voice. I opened my eyes and adjusted them for a second as last night's sexual ecstasy came rushing back to me.

I turned and realised Francesco wasn't in the bed, it was him talking on the phone in the kitchen. I got myself up, already dressed as we had fallen asleep with half our clothes on. I walked to him to find him on the phone, and as he looked up at me, he looked alarmed.

He was speaking fast and low. There must be news I thought. As I waited for him to finish his call I made my coffee, picking up a few words here and there from his conversation without meaning to eavesdrop. He hung up.

"Is everything ok?" I asked.

He sighed. "Yes, well, no" he said, "I have to back to Italy for a few days. They've had the autopsy results and they've confirmed she's drowned, but her family aren't convinced and want to run more tests. They want me to go as the police have a few more questions". He bowed his head over the counter, holding the phone.

I felt so sorry for him in that moment, I wished I could take his pain away. I wished this had never happened.
"I was thinking..." he said, "What if you came with me?"

"Came with you?" I replied surprised, "To Italy?"

"I know it's short notice and it's a crazy idea, but it would only be for a few days and honestly I don't want to be apart again" he said.
He sounded so defeated. Quite frankly I didn't want to go, to be the new girlfriend. Everyone would judge him and me.
"Do you think it's appropriate though?" I said, "I mean, this is your ex that's died, and then you bring your new girlfriend, it's a bit, I don't know, awkward?".
"It is" he said, "but I can deal with the family and police, and then we'll have some time to be together. I can show you where I'm from, show you around. It would definitely be a good distraction for me. It's been great here with you the last few days, its really helped. And also, you're my fiancé... not my girlfriend". He smiled. I melted.

"Well, I'll have to sort things out with Kat, but ok..why not!" I said.

"Great!" he said, "I'll start looking for tickets. We can leave today if there's flights available?"

"Ok" I said, "let's do it".

What was I thinking jetting off with him in the middle of this massive investigation and putting myself in the middle – with this guy I barely knew? Well, you are engaged to him I reminded myself.
This was insane ...but I really didn't want him to leave. What was the worst that could happen? It might be nice to visit his home, let him show me around, plus we could get some ideas for the wedding and maybe talk about a date? I was getting ahead of myself I thought, as usual.

Francesco found us flights for that evening, and so I spent the day getting organised with Kat about the shop and packing my suitcase. We would only be gone for 3 days so I didn't need much, but with my overpacking issues taking over, I had stuffed quite a lot in. We booked a taxi to the airport and left late that afternoon. By that evening we were on a plane to Italy.

Chapter 18

We landed late and the airport and the whole vibe kept reminding me of the last time I was here and being stood up. I had to push it to the back of mind otherwise it would ruin the whole trip. I was apprehensive and followed him through the airport and out to grab a taxi. After a long taxi ride, we arrived to his house and it wasn't as I had imagined. It was a modern little house in the city, similar to mine but with more character, I guess it being Italian it made it all the nicer.

Inside was pretty nice, small but nice, although not overly decorated. One bedroom, one small kitchen and living room combined, and one small bathroom. I put my things in the bedroom.

"Sorry about this" he said, as he rushed to change the sheets on the bed. "I didn't think I would be coming back with someone, so never changed them before I left." As he ran around getting clean sheets and changing the bed, I had a look around.

"Nice place" I said.

"It does the job" he said laughing, "Not much to look at, but the location is great".

"Hmm" I said and continued my tour of the house. When I got back to the bedroom, he had just about finished placing the last blanket on top of the bed.

"There" he said, "perfect". I smiled and sat on the bed, taking off my shoes.

"You must be tired" he said.
"I am" I said and laid on the bed. "Maybe we should go to sleep? What's your plan for tomorrow?"

"Tomorrow morning I'll leave early and go talk to the police, stay here and I'll be back early. I'll make sure you have everything you need. Afterwards we can have a walk around if you like?" he said.

"Sounds good" I said. I was excited to be here with him, although the circumstances were not the happiest. I got ready for bed and tucked myself in just in time to see him stripping to his boxers.
My gaze on him, I enjoyed watching him and my mind took me back to the night before. I felt my cheeks flush. He slid in the bed, pulling the cover over himself.
"What a long day" he said sighing, "I'm glad you're here though". He turned to face me, and I smiled.

"Me too" I said.

I looked into his eyes, his gorgeous eyes, his soulful eyes. I leaned in and kissed him. He cupped my face and kissed me back, deepening the kiss, our tongues intertwined, our breathing becoming heavier as if we couldn't get enough of each other. I reached my hand down and felt his cock, hard, it excited me. I caressed him over his boxers before pulling them down and moving on top of him. I kissed him and caressed his tongue with mine. I held his cock in my hand and guided him towards my pussy. Slowly I pushed him inside of me, sitting on top of him, feeling him fully. I arched my back, I couldn't catch my breath, I had him yet wanted him so badly. I moved up and down, back and forth, thrusting him inside me over and over, faster and faster.

His hands held on to my hips as he moved with me. "Fuck" he said softly, "fuck I'm going to come", and with that he tilted his head back and moaned. I slowed down, letting him savour his release. He looked back at me, his eyes wide, as his breathing slowed down.

He grabbed my hips once more and maneuvered me back on the bed laying down, as he towered on top of me. He kissed me. He stopped and raised his hand to my face. He traced his middle finger across my lips. I parted them instinctively and with that his finger slid inside my mouth. He pushed it fully in. "Mmm" I said and sucked him as he moved it out and back in once more. I watched him as I sucked. He pulled his finger out and reached down, brushing past my clit and then entering me with it. I gasped and closed my eyes. One finger, then two, I moaned. He moved his head to my chest and put my nipple in his mouth, his tongue flicking around it over and over, while his fingers still inside me, I came.

I woke up the next morning and Francesco wasn't there; he wasn't in the bed. I got up and went to the kitchen and there was a pot of freshly made coffee and a note. It read: I didn't want to wake you, I'll be back soon. Enjoy your coffee and make yourself at home.

Ok I thought, I need a coffee, glad to have a minute to myself. Everything was happening so fast and last night, God last night, and the night before, and the proposal. My head was spinning. I poured myself a cup and sat at the small kitchen table, looking out the window. I got lost in my thoughts. What was I doing? Was everything ok with Francesco? Was everything ok with the police? I finished my coffee and messaged Francesco: Hope everything is, ok? Just going to hop in the bath while I wait x

I went into the bedroom and undressed, opening my suitcase to choose my clothes for the day. I went into the bathroom and found a clean towel. I stared at the taps in the bath and wondered if there was enough hot water, as I could have really done with a long one to relax.

My phone pinged and I went to check it in the bedroom. It was from Francesco: Hey! almost done, I'll be home soon. Better if you take a shower, the bathtub isn't in good condition x

Right, shower then, maybe he has a leaky bath. By the time I was ready and dressed Francesco was back.

"Hey" he said as he walked in.

"How was it?" I asked.

"It went fine, I cleared up a few more things with the police, just formalities. Even though we know what she died of though, the family still want further tests to be run. I guess they just won't accept she did this to herself" he said.

"Oh, that's sad" I said, "they must not be able to deal with that, will you go see them?"

"I will before we leave, just to say goodbye" he said.

We spent the next couple of days looking around as he showed me his favourite spots, the food was incredible, and I was so glad I had come. Francesco always had his camera with him, snapping away wherever we went. When it was our last day, he wanted to go say his goodbyes to the family before we went to the airport. "I won't be long" he said.

"Ok, I'll wait for you here" I said, "it'll give me time to get ready and finish packing. Hey, I forgot to ask, what's up with the bath? I really could have used a long one the other day".

"Ah" he said, "yeah, well back in the day when I was starting out in photography, I kind of used the bath as a makeshift developer and the bathroom as a dark room." He laughed, "I was poor. Even put a red bulb in and everything"

"Right" I said laughing.

"So, let's just say the chemicals I used in that tub, well, I wouldn't bathe in there ever again" he said chuckling.

"Ok, I won't take the chance" I said smiling.

He headed off and I took my shower, alone with my thoughts. At least he was getting his closure being here. Once we left, he could start to process what had happened. As our time in Italy was coming to an end, I looked forward to being back home. I had wanted to bring up the wedding so many times but didn't feel it was right to talk
about the future, a happy occasion, when he was dealing with all this.
When would we set a date? Where would we do it? I let myself imagine a wedding dress and him in a suit, how happy it made me. I was also afraid if I mentioned a wedding, he would think it was too soon to talk about. Granted, he had asked me to marry him after barely any time together, but I didn't want to risk anything.
Within a day of being back home he received news of a freelance job, working out in Germany. He would be gone at least a week.
We hadn't spoken about our living circumstances yet; would he move in with me officially? Would he keep his house in Italy? It felt like we were just going with the flow, and I didn't want to start interrogating him. I wanted to keep this easy-going vibe. He left for Germany.

"See you next week" he said as he kissed me goodbye. I returned to work the next day and it gave me some muchneeded stability after these hectic last couple of weeks. I regaled Kat with my gossip, and forgetting I had my engagement ring on, eagle eyed Kat pounced on me with a million questions. When I told her he had proposed, she was speechless.

"But you haven't even known him that long!" she said. "I know" I said, "it's insane, it's almost ridiculous, but it feels right".

"It feels right" she said, "but I mean, who proposes after a few weeks? I can't believe it" she kept saying over and over.

I calmed her down and she said that if I was happy, it was the main thing, but to keep my guard up. I reassured her that I would.

"Plus, you'll get to be bridesmaid" I said smiling.

"Only if I get to choose the dress!" she laughed back.

"Of course," I said, "I wouldn't have it any other way!"

We spent the next week talking excitedly about the wedding, what it should be like, what it should look like. I was getting ahead of myself but loved talking about it, loved imagining it, the cheesiness of it all.

I spoke with Francesco every day; we would message all day and talk on the phone at night.

There hadn't been word from Italy since we left, about the findings of the further testing, so the conversation turned lighter as the days passed as it was mentioned less and less.

I had planned to talk to him about the wedding when he returned. Was he really serious about it all? Did he still want me to be his wife? I hoped that as time had passed it hadn't given him second thoughts, it had been so impulsive after all. What a fool I would feel like if he realised he had been too hasty, while I was still full steam ahead on the whole thing. Although the week passed quickly as work kept me occupied, I missed him and his touch. I missed sleeping in bed with him and making love. Occasionally our messages got flirtier than usual, what he would like to do to me, what I would like to do to him, what we would do once he came back. Sometimes it got too much, and I pleasured myself to the memories of our lovemaking as they came to me in fragments.
The licking, the touching, his eyes, his scent. I would inevitably come quickly, leaving me more frustrated than before, as I wanted him in the flesh and not in my imagination.

Finally, the day came, and he was due back. He was arriving in the evening which gave me time to get ready at home after work, while I eagerly waited.

The knock at the door came, and even though I had been pacing around the house waiting, I didn't want to open the door too fast, trying to be as casual as I could. I waited for what seemed like forever, when all I probably mustered was a few seconds, before hurriedly walking to the door and opening it.

With a whoosh of air there he was, his silhouette standing there, his coat, his face, his hair. I felt my heart in my throat. He smiled a big smile and embraced me as I pulled him inside and shut the door behind him. Dropping his bag at his feet we kissed, slowly at first and then more passionately. He cupped my face, and I ran my hand through his hair, grabbing his soft curls, intertwining them through my fingers and tugging them gently. I breathed him in.
Suddenly I had an idea, and with my heart racing, I pulled away from him. I looked into his eyes for a moment.

"Kneel" I whispered, as I kept eye contact with him and tried to remain expressionless. His eyes flickered with delight and a smile escaped him. He waited a moment, processing it, smiling. He slowly lowered himself to his knees, lifting his head upwards, staring at me. He licked his lips. I pulled up my dress and hooked my fingers through my underwear.
I slowly pulled them down and off my legs, watching him watching me. I pulled my skirt up again, gathering it and holding it in one hand, as my other hand reached for his hair, his curls. I grabbed a fistful and pulled him gently towards me. Resting my knee over his shoulder, I moved my pelvis towards his face and pressed him into my pussy. As I felt his touch a moan escaped me involuntarily. His lips kissed my clitoris, then his tongue danced over it. I closed my eyes in ecstasy.
I moved his head gently and tugged harder at his hair. "Mmm" he groaned. I looked down at him, flushed. I could barely speak. "Show me how much you like tasting me" I whispered. He eyes shot up to mine, and as he continued licking me, he smiled. I felt his teeth against my pussy and moaned again.

I felt his body move as he fumbled with his jean's buttons. He parted his mouth from my pussy and stood on his knees for a second as he swiftly pulled down his jeans and boxers, his cock hard. He quickly knelt back in position and continued to tease me with his tongue, his hand now gripping his cock as he caressed himself back and forth. To see him was bliss. "Mmm" I moaned again. Moving my pelvis back and forth, my pussy against his wet mouth, I could feel myself building to orgasm and my breathing quickened once more. "Dirty girl" he whispered suddenly, and with that my body took over and exploded. "Mmm, ah!" he cried as he came, panting, resting his head against my thigh.
As I calmed down, I moved my leg off his shoulder, and let my skirt fall over my hips.
He sat for a second. "Nice to see you again" he said smiling. I laughed and he stood up, his legs wobbly. Remembering my own wobbly legs from not long ago, I couldn't help but love that I done the same to him.

We gathered ourselves. He unpacked and told me about his trip. We sat down to dinner, drinking and talking, and I thought the time was right.

"So, I don't know if you've given any thought to this" I said, "and I completely understand it if you haven't, given everything that you've been dealing with, but, do you know or have an idea of when you'd like .."

"Spit it out!" he said laughing.

"The wedding" I blurted out, "the wedding, a wedding, I mean, we are engaged, unless you've changed your mind? I mean if you don't want to talk about it I understand it's just I was-"

"Hey" he said, "don't be so nervous! Of course, I've thought about it, I've asked you to marry me, to be my wife, and I haven't changed my mind. Miriam, I've never felt like this with anyone, it's you I want, it's you, my love".

I blushed and prayed he couldn't see it.

"Don't blush" he said, reaching out to touch my cheek. We both laughed.

"I don't know about you" he said, "but I'd like to marry you as soon as possible"
"Why didn't you say anything before?!" I said.

"Well, I didn't want to scare you away, I thought maybe I'd give you some time in case, I don't know, I guess we were both impulsive. I didn't want to push you; you might have had only said yes in the heat of the moment".

I smiled. "No, I've never felt like this either" I said, "I want to marry you, now, tomorrow. Let's elope for all I care; I just want you".

He leaned over. "I want you too" he whispered and pressed his lips against mine.

Chapter 19

As the days passed, we discussed a wedding and concluded that we didn't want a big affair, we just wanted to be married. Why didn't we just do it at city hall, book into a nice hotel afterwards and just have a fun day, no pressure, no mess. I quite liked that idea as I really didn't want to think about sending out invitations to people who didn't even know I was with someone and having to explain – plus there was Lorenzo. Did I really want to send invitations out to mutual friends, he would be devastated. At least if it was done under the radar, he wouldn't learn about it straight away. I would invite Kat as my bridesmaid and witness. I didn't need anyone else there.

"Let's check when their next available appointment is" Francesco said, talking about city hall. I opened their webpage and navigated to wedding registration.

"Next week" I said, "or one month from now". I looked up at him and he smiled.

"What are your plans for next week?" he said grinning.

"I don't know" I replied, "I think I might be getting married". We both laughed as he rushed towards me and scooped me up in his arms.

"Come with me, wife!" he said loudly, still grinning, as he carried me to the bedroom and dropped me on the bed. Laughing as I bounced, he cupped my face in his hands and kissed me, his tongue pushing its way into my mouth with intention. "Mm" he said as he pulled away.

Suddenly he placed his hands on my hips and swivelled me around, my chest now pressing against the mattress. I felt my skirt being pulled up. He quickly and roughly slid my underwear down to my ankles. For a brief second nothing happened, and then a jolt, as I felt his cock against my ass, pushing, rubbing me up and down. "Mm" I moaned as I buried my head on the bed and closed my eyes. His cock made its way down to my pussy, rubbing. He entered me, thrusting himself inside of me all at once. "Ah" I gasped, as he pulled himself out and thrust again, this time harder. I gasped again.

I felt him lean forward and then his hand in my hair, grabbing a fistful. He pulled himself out and as he tugged my hair back gently, he thrust himself inside me once more. I moaned. I wanted him to do as he pleased with me, my body was his. He leaned forward again, resting his chest on my back, and with another tug of my hair I felt his lips on my neck and then his teeth, a soft bite. "Mmmm" I whispered breathlessly. I reached my hand back and grabbed his hair, tugging at it roughly, squeezing it. "Aaah" he whispered as he thrust inside me again, moving faster now.

His lips still on my neck, he bit again, this time a little harder. I cried out, the sensation, the pain mixing with the pleasure, heightening all of it. I wanted him to bite harder, I wanted to bite him. I tugged his hair in response. He groaned, thrusting in and out of me, holding on to my hair, tightening his grip. "Mmmmm" he moaned and stilled as he came, letting his head fall on my shoulder.

Loosening his grip on my hair, I was still breathing fast, my clitoris throbbing. I felt his body lift itself off me and then his lips on my back, kissing me. His kisses making their way down my back, further and further, until he reached my ass.

His lips on my cheeks, and suddenly a little bite, a lick with his tongue and more kissing, little kisses. I felt his mouth between my cheeks, kissing, licking. I pushed my ass upwards involuntarily, my body writhing with anticipation. His kisses made their way down. I inhaled sharply, feeling his warm wet tongue on my asshole, as he caressed it slowly. I pressed myself against him, relishing the sensation, feeling my face hot and red. I gasped again as I felt his finger reach underneath me, on my clit, rubbing. I moved with him, my body grinding. Moaning as his tongue licked my ass and his finger massaged my clit. I let out a long moan as my body trembled and came hard, shaking from the intensity. It washed over me, over and over, wave after wave. My mind empty, reeling. My breath jagged and heavy. I kept my eyes closed, I didn't want to open them, I wanted to stay in that moment.

"You're so beautiful" he whispered, kissing my neck. Still with my eyes shut, I felt the warmth of his lips and his scent, our sweaty bodies intertwined.

The next week seemed to fly past as we got ready for the wedding, well, if you could call it a wedding that is. Kat was anxious, she was hesitant about the whole thing but excited none the less as she helped me plan the details. She came with me to pick out a dress in one of the local stores. "I'm not sure I want a proper wedding dress" I said, "I mean it's not a typical wedding".

"Well, that, and should you be wearing white?" she giggled I laughed.

"Well, let's see what they have" I said.
As I scoured the store, I didn't see anything I liked and we made our way to a bunch of different ones. We went into a second-hand shop on a whim and there, as I rummaged through the densely packed hangers, I saw it. It was a white silk dress, simple, but so beautiful.

"I'm going to try this one on" I said loudly to Kat, who was at the other end of the aisle looking at some stripy beetlejuice type pants – if anyone could pull those off it was her, I thought as I made my way down to the changing room. The dress was my size, but would it fit nicely? These types of dresses usually hugged me in all the wrong places, but it was so beautiful I had to try.
In my bra and undies, I carefully took the straps off the hanger and lifted the dress over my head. As I pulled the fabric down, the silk felt soft and slippery. I was expecting it to get stuck somehow but as the material fell over my hips I was surprised. It was loose, comfortable and it fit me. Ok it fits but it probably looks like shit I thought, seeing only the top half in the cracked shop mirror.
I made my way out of the changing room to the floor length mirror outside. As I saw my reflection my heart skipped a beat, and I knew this was it. This was the dress. I didn't think in a million years I would ever look good in a dress like this, but there it was. The silk fabric had a slight sheen, the neck was scooped so it was low but not too low, showing of my collar bone and neck. The straps were thin and framed my shoulders.
The hem fell to just above ankle length. It was gorgeous and I felt beautiful. Kat appeared in the mirror as I saw her walking up being me, her jaw dropped.

"Wow" she said as she stopped beside me. "Wow" she said again.

"I think I'll take this one" I said smiling.
"If you don't, I'll have to force it on you" she said laughing, "this one is perfect, you look stunning". I blushed and looked at my reflection again. This is the dress I'll be wearing when I marry Francesco I thought. I couldn't believe it was really happening.

I paid for the dress, and we made our way out, spending the rest of the day shopping and chatting, feeling giddy. Francesco had sourced a suit. He kept it wrapped and hidden in the closet and wouldn't let me see it. I hid my dress too, wanting to keep it a surprise for him. As the day drew nearer, I had butterflies in my stomach, I was walking on air. Time flew and moved at a snail's pace all in one go. I was so in love, so complete, so fulfilled.

The morning finally came, our appointment at city hall was at 2 pm and I would meet Francesco there. He took his suit that morning and made his way to the hotel he had booked for our wedding night, leaving me to get ready back at home. Kat was coming over to help with my hair. I showered, washed my hair and with my bathrobe on I started to apply my make up. Nothing over the top, just subtle, a nice rosy glow. As I was almost finished Kat arrived, hair curler in one hand and champagne in the other.

"Eeek!!" we both cried as I opened the door.

"Wedding day!!" she said excitedly and made her way to the cupboard to get some glasses for the champagne.

"I can't believe it's finally here" I said.

"I know" she said, "I'm so happy for you. But Miriam, promise me you'll be careful".

"I will" I said rolling my eyes.
"Ok c'mon" she said, pouring two glasses of champagne,
"let's go get your hair sorted!"

We giggled and giggled as Kat did my hair, lovely loose curls. At one point I thought I would have to redo my makeup as I kept laughing into my champagne glass making the drink spurt everywhere. I was on a high and I was so grateful Kat was there to share it with me. When she finished my hair, she grabbed my dress hanging on the back of the door and laid it out on the bed.

"You're going to look stunning" she said.

As I looked down at the dress, I felt my stomach flip. This was it. I took it carefully and went into the bathroom to change, taking off my bath robe and carefully slipping the dress over my head, trying my best not to ruin the hairstyle or have the makeup rub off on it – that would be just typical I thought. It felt just as it had when I tried it on at the shop, it fit like a glove and with the hair and makeup it just brought everything together. I felt amazing, I felt beautiful and couldn't wait to see Francescos reaction. I couldn't wait to see his suit either, or rather the suit I would be peeling off him in our hotel room tonight. He would look good in anything anyway I thought. I stepped out into the bedroom and Kats expression said it all. Her eyes glistened.

"Are you going to cry?!" I said.

"I'm not crying, you are" she said laughing and wiped a tear away. "He's lucky to have you" she said.

"Thanks Kat" I said and hugged her.

"I'll wait for you in the kitchen" she said, as I started grabbing my shoes and bag to get ready to go.

"Ok hon! Be there in a sec!" I said.

I looked for my phone, it was here somewhere amongst the mess of hair tools, clothes and champagne glasses. I finally found it under my makeup bag. I flicked it on and had a message from Francesco: I'm at the hotel x

I hadn't checked my phone since I started getting ready, had it been that long already, I smiled to myself. As I exited out of the messages, I noticed a notification from the Sicilian local newspaper. I had set up notifications in case there was any news on the case, back when his ex-girlfriend was missing, and we were waiting for news. It must have been an update to say they were running more tests on the body I thought, as I clicked into the link.

 Using google translate I read the article:

Medical examiner finds traces of acetic acid in water found in the lungs of Martina Daak. A spokesperson for the Police made this statement today: we conducted further testing as per the request of the family of the deceased. After testing the water that was found in the lungs of Martina Daak, a trace of acetic acid has been found. These traces do not match samples of the water taken from the river where her body was found, therefore we believe that she drowned elsewhere and was placed in the river postmortem. We are upgrading our investigation to homicide and if anyone has any information, please contact us directly.

Acetic acid? I thought. What the heck is that? Had Francesco seen the news? This would re-open everything back up again. Oh god, what could have happened to her? He would be devastated when he found out. He had been convinced that she had drowned herself.

Acetic acid, I thought again. This makes no sense. I opened a google search, typed in the words and hit search.

"Hey! Not getting cold feet, are you?!" Kat bellowed.

"No No!" I shouted back, "I'm coming!"

I read down through the search results, not seeing anything that would explain this. As I scrolled and tried to understand what it was used for, one result caught my eye. Acetic acid, a chemical involved in the developing of film ... I stopped reading. My heart thumped. Developing of film, photographs ... As my brain connected the dots, I suddenly remembered the bathtub. His bathtub in his house. I couldn't use it because he had used it for .... developing photographs.

Wait, what? I thought. Where else could acetic acid be found? How could it be in water that she drowned in? This made no sense; he couldn't be linked. My heart dropped. I felt sick and my mouth was dry.
Did I really think he had done something here? There had to be an explanation, a logical explanation. But could I really say I knew him? I tried to focus. I remembered all the interviews with the police, how he had been so involved in the whole case from the beginning. I tried to replay all our conversations about the case and still couldn't see any red flags, anything that might seem strange now.

He had changed his number and come straight here after he had found out she wasn't pregnant, could something have happened then? What if he had done something? In the heat of the moment, maybe there had been an accident? My thoughts came back to today, the wedding. I remembered how my life had been just a few months before I had met him, how mundane it was, how I had wished for something more. Now I had what I wanted but there were so still so many questions.
All the ups and downs, the lies. I was mixed up in a murder investigation for God's sake, and now, well now I was on my way to my own wedding, and I wasn't even sure I knew who my future husband really was. I believed deep down he wouldn't ever be capable of something as grotesque as murder, but could I live with the small doubt? I loved him, but was that enough?

I was jolted out of my thoughts as I heard Kat from the kitchen. "Well, c'mon!" she shouted, "We're gonna be late!"

Suddenly my phone pinged. I looked at the screen and it was a message from Francesco.

Can't wait to marry you, Mrs Barone..

To be continued..